JEAN AINLEY: Her fledgling company, Executive Meals Service, was finally taking off. But while Jean could whip up a sublime soufflé or produce perfect Scotch eggs, solving a murder was a little out of her league.

ONGAR MANGANIAN: Behind his back he was called the Starving Armenian. Jean discovered that Manganian's hunger was even greater than it seemed . . .

ALDO UCCELLO: Manganian called Aldo his "Personal Assistant." Jean thought "Official Taster" was more like it— until she saw Aldo display a surprising show of muscle . . .

GRETEL: Her father didn't want his daughter to become an au pair. So he enrolled her as an apprentice in Jean's catering service, and Gretel proceeded to wreck havoc.

LEXIE: Jean's comely blond apprentice was a minor socialite with visions of grandeur. She had a habit of undoing buttons when wealthy men were being served.

★

"A cheery tale. . . . This funny, clever thriller . . . blends Emma Lathen's knowledge of high-finance high jinks with Julia Child's cooking expertise."

—Booklist

"Books of marvelous versatility . . . [with] flashes of delicious humor . . . Marian Babson's crime novels have gone from strength to strength."

—Twentieth Century Crime & Mystery Writers

ALSO BY MARIAN BABSON

BEJEWELLED DEATH
THE CRUISE OF A DEATHTIME
DEATH BESIDE THE SEA
FATAL FORTUNE
A FOOL FOR MURDER
GUILTY PARTY
LINE UP FOR MURDER
PRETTY LADY

PUBLISHED BY
WARNER BOOKS

MARIAN BABSON

DEATH WARMED UP

WARNER BOOKS

A Time Warner Company

WARNER BOOKS EDITION

Copyright © 1992 by Marian Babson
All rights reserved.

Cover design by Jackie Merri Meyer
Cover illustration by Phillip Singer

This Warner Books Edition is published by arrangement with William
Collins Sons & Co. Ltd.

Warner Books, Inc.
1271 Avenue of the Americas
New York, NY 10020

 A Time Warner Company

Printed in the United States of America

First Warner Books Printing: January, 1994

10 9 8 7 6 5 4 3 2 1

DEATH WARMED UP

Chapter
1

The mayonnaise had curdled, the stove had conked out with the meal half-cooked and the soufflé had never had a chance.

I stood in the midst of desolation and silently cursed the day Nick had persuaded me that the path to financial salvation would be lined with deb-types queueing up for special tuition (apprentice was such a down market term) with a first-class private catering service. These days, the smart money no longer went on curtseying to Queen Charlotte's Birthday Cake, but on learning how to make one.

"Oh, Jean! Jean—" Lexie hurled herself at me from the far corner of the room. "I don't know what went wrong! I only turned my back for the teeniest possible minute—I had to go to the loo—and when I came back—"

Whereas I had been gone for nearly half an hour. I had been on the telephone firming up the details on a Boardroom luncheon for twenty-five in the City next Thursday. It had taken longer than I had expected since every query ("Gas or electricity?") had revealed further problems. ("Well, neither, really—not for cooking. Of course, we have electricity. I mean, we have this super oak-panelled Boardroom, but...")

More by divination than information given, I had ascertained that there were no cooking facilities on the premises and no means to accommodate any. Therefore a cold buffet would have to be the order of the day. By the time I had settled this, and with the strong feeling that I had just been dragged through a hedge backwards, I had come back upstairs to face chaos.

"All right, all right. No time for that—" I thrust Lexie away from me. With any encouragement at all, she would have sunk to a shuddering heap at my feet, wailing out her distress. (Really, she ought to have been enrolled in the Royal Academy of Dramatic Art. Except, of course, that cooking was a more demonstrable and marketable skill in this day and age than the mere ability to declaim. Far better to be able to whip up a soufflé than a scene.)

I noted with approval that her friend and co-apprentice, Sidonie, had unearthed an eggbeater, a carton of whipping cream and a half-bottle of brandy from our emergency basket and was eyeing the chocolate *appareil au soufflé* with a determined expression. That girl had the right idea: load the pudding with enough booze and the Board of Directors would think they were getting the real goods. They weren't gourmets—they only liked to think they were.

"Come on—" I rallied Lexie. "It's salvage time. We'll have the post-mortems later."

How could I have known that it was such an unfortunate choice of words?

My main concern was to snatch—if not triumph—at least an edible meal from the ruination around me.

It would be putting it too strongly to suggest that the success of the proposed merger depended upon the meal set before Ongar Manganian, but it was certain that he would be better able to judge the quality thereof than any of the whisky-blasted palates possessed by some of the Board of Directors of Quardon International. Behind his back (if gossip columns could be so described), he was often referred to as "the Starving Armenian," as much because of his gargantuan appetite for food, wine and women as because of his antecedents.

Nevertheless, I had known of at least one promising business deal which had sunk without trace when a short sharp burst of ptomaine had followed immediately upon the presumed-nuptial meal. When the tycoon being wooed had been released from hospital after having had his stomach pumped, he had been unavailable to his suitor-company for evermore.

It was more than that, of course. It was also a matter of personal pride and a sense of gratitude. Quardon International was our oldest and most reliable client. Their monthly luncheons helped to balance our books. They paid promptly and even said thank-you occasionally.

Furthermore, we wished to retain their custom if the proposed merger with Ongar Manganian's English company went through.

I lifted the lid of the fish kettle to check on the progress of the poached salmon; it was now cooling rapidly in its court bouillon, but appeared to be sufficiently cooked. Thank heavens for that. Without heat, I could not transform the court bouillon into the sauce I had intended but fortunately Lexie had made—or tried to make—mayonnaise for those who might prefer it. That could still be salvaged, but did I trust Lexie to do it?

Probably not. I took a clean basin and mixed half a teaspoon of mustard into a very thin cream with water, then began adding the curdled sauce, drop by drop. Lexie watched me closely.

"Are you all right up here?" Edda Price, Tristram Quardon's secretary, hurried into the kitchen, panting slightly.

"Yes, fine," I lied, moving defensively to block her view. I noticed with approval that Sidonie had also changed position so that her activities were unobservable.

"You are?" Edda's voice reflected doubt. "If so, you're the only ones. We haven't an electric typewriter working in the building. The lifts are out, too."

She flicked the wall switch. No lights went on.

"There!" she said. "I thought so. It's just not good enough! I shall get on to the Electricity Board immediately. They really must warn us in advance when they're planning a power cut!"

I was aware of the swift relieved glances passing between Lexie and Sidonie. It was all the fault of a power cut. They could not be blamed in any way for the oven's having lost heat at a crucial moment.

"How long has the electricity been off?" I asked.

"I've no idea. It's lunch hour for the staff, so no one was trying to type. And the day is so bright and sunny, there weren't many lights on." She gave an approving glance skywards through the window. "Spring's coming."

Fluffy white clouds scudded across a bright blue sky propelled by a brisk wind with a touch of softness in it. I had noticed it myself this morning as I started out and had the same thought. Spring was on the way.

So was Quarter Day and all the bills.

"What time did the clocks stop?" Sidonie spoke for the first time, cutting straight to the core of the situation in her usual incisive way. She was the serious side of the dazzling beauty/plain practical girl combination one so often sees in best friends at that age. She did not, I noticed thankfully, pause in her labours with eggbeater, brandy and cream. Lexie would always try to get round a difficult situation— even a culinary one—by undoing a couple more buttons and breathing deeply. Sidonie knew only too well that a lot more effort would be demanded from her.

"Of course! I hadn't thought of the clocks!" Edda Price darted out into the corridor and we heard her clatter down one flight of stairs. There was nothing so vulgar as an electric clock mounted on any wall in the Executive Suite. If they had attained the cachet of taking lunch in the dining-room up here, they were above mere clock-watching.

"Don't open the fridge!" I warned sharply as Lexie made a move in that direction. It couldn't do the chilled melon any harm, but we'd want to slide Sidonie's confection inside and had better retain as much coldness as possible. There was no telling how much longer the Directors would linger over their drinks or how long the power cut would last. With the kind of luck we were having today, I didn't want to take chances.

"That's all right!" Edda Price bustled back into the tiny kitchen heaving a sigh of relief. "The power's only been off for half an hour. It must have happened just after the Board meeting broke up. They won't have noticed anything and we won't need lights in the dining-room today. I shall go and complain to the Electricity Board at once! If they restore the power as soon as possible, the lifts should be working again by the time luncheon is over and the Directors want to leave."

"The kitchen equipment—" I began. But I was speaking to her departing back. She hadn't heard me and it hadn't occurred to her that the oven, the fridge, the dishwasher and all the ancillary equipment ran on electricity. She was worried about the electric typewriters and the lifts; things more immediately concerned with the Directors' interests. I wondered how long it would take her to realize that a ruined lunch might be considered an inconvenience to them.

"That's funny." Lexie had wandered over and was looking out of the window. "Everything seems to be working in the offices across the street."

"So it does." I joined her and we stood watching the activity within our range of vision. Typewriter carriages moved briskly, computer screens glowed, lights flicked on and off at desks as people moved purposefully, returning from lunch or just leaving for it. "Perhaps they're on a different section of the grid."

"Perhaps." She moved closer to the glass and leaned her forehead against it, twisting to look up and down the street on our side. "But nothing seems to be happening. I mean, when there's a power cut, staff usually take advantage of it and pop out *en masse* to do a bit of shopping. Nobody minds because there's nothing else they can do. But it's all quiet below and—'' She craned for a better view. "And I'm *sure* I can see the reflection of lights next door."

"Well, that doesn't help us any." I moved away from the window. "Unless you were thinking of popping next door and asking them if we could use their cooker—if they have one."

"Wouldn't you just know—" Lexie sighed heavily "—that this would happen to *us*?"

It wasn't the worst thing that had ever happened to her—not by a long shot. However, it was interesting to note that she was aligning herself so thoroughly with Executive Meal Service. I had heard her refer to it, when she didn't know I was listening, as "Meals for Wheels"—a name which was also creeping into occasional business slang. No bad thing, really, to have a catchy nickname. In these sorts of circles, it was half the publicity battle won. But if the meals weren't top quality, no amount of publicity could keep the business afloat.

Sidonie had done a magnificent job. The erstwhile soufflé base was transformed with cream and brandy, topped with whipped cream and sprinkled with crystallized violets. Now we could risk opening the fridge to pop it inside and trust that it would have attained a suitable degree of chill by the time the Directors were ready for it.

What we would do for hot coffee without any electricity, I didn't know. Perhaps, if we were very lucky, the power might be restored before it was time to serve the coffee. Alternatively, I might ring Mona and have her prepare a portable urn of coffee there and send Lexie or Sidonie in the van to collect it.

"Stand by," I warned Sidonie, picking up her dessert creation. "Open the fridge door for me—no wider than you have to—and slam it shut again as soon as I pop this inside."

"Right." She moved over to the fridge and we executed the manoeuvre with perfect teamwork. It was disconcerting to see the fridge dark; one doesn't realize how much unconscious cheer that tiny light at the back radiates.

"I can hear them coming!" Lexie's voice rose on a note of hysteria. "They're ready to eat! What shall we do?"

"Feed them," Sidonie said practically.

"Hell!" I dashed next door to the dining-room to check that everything was in order. Lexie had set the table and was sometimes inclined to be a bit scatty about such things, although she could usually be depended upon to pay proper attention to the food itself.

All was well, however. White linen napkins folded into water-lily shapes swam on gleaming plates; the proper place setting was set round every place; the flower arrangement in the centre of the table was fragrant, springlike and, most important, low enough so that they could talk to one another across it.

I lit the candles flanking the flower arrangement, conscious of the voices approaching as the Directors came down the corridor from the Boardroom at the far end. Next to the Boardroom was a small well-stocked bar, to which they adjourned at the end of Board meetings, and for which I was thankful. It kept them out of our hair until they were actually ready to be seated for their meal. In companies without such an amenity, they came directly into the dining-room and served themselves from a bar on a small table set up in a corner, then roamed all over the dining-room with their drinks, getting underfoot while we tried to work.

One final look: everything okay. I dashed back to the kitchen, ignoring the knot gathered outside a small door midway along the corridor, playing their usual game of "After you, Gaston" and trying to look as though they weren't queueing for the use of the Executive Loo.

Because I was still looking back over my shoulder, trying to see if Tristram Quardon was coming, I collided with the man in the centre of the kitchen. I would have collided with him no matter where he stood. It was a small room and he seemed to fill it, pushing Lexie and Sidonie into corners. He

was a great bear of a man, one of those larger-than-life
grotesques that life occasionally throws off. They are often
to be seen in the most successful ranks of business, politics,
or whatever—perhaps in sheer self-defence.

"Oh-ho! little ones!" He caught me and held me off at
arm's length, which meant I just barely cleared his enormous girth. "More speed, less haste, no? Or is it the other
way around?" His laugh boomed out, shaking the bottles of
wine which were open and supposed to be breathing quietly
on the sideboard. I could only hope the sediment wasn't
stirred and decided that it might be safe to decant it before
serving. The Directors were rather more knowledgeable
about their drink than their food.

"And what do you do here?" A gold tooth glinted in the
corner of his smile. His beard was an untidy Van Dyke
which threatened, like everything else about him, to burst
its bounds at any moment.

"Be nice to her," Lexie said pertly. "She's the boss."

"Oh-ho." The small shrewd eyes sparkled beneath the
shaggy overhanging eyebrows. "Then it is to you I complain if I do not like the meal?"

"*If* . . ." I tried to smile. It was not comforting to know
that his mind was running along such lines before he even
sat down at the table. I wondered how the Board meeting
had gone. If they were all in a bad mood, it would be easier
for them to blame the food for their discontent than themselves.

"There you are, Ongar." Tristram Quardon spoke from
the doorway behind me. "You haven't seen Mark Avery
anywhere, have you?"

"Would I be likely to?" Ongar Manganian released me in
order to spread his arms wide in a huge shrug. "That man
does not like me, my friend. He does not approve of our
deal. There were moments in the Boardroom this morning
when I thought he was going to issue the ultimatum that the
merger would proceed only over his dead body. I am still
not so sure that he will not find some way to block it."

"You mustn't pay too much attention to what Mark says

right now." Tristram Quardon was patently uncomfortable. He too seemed to wish that Ongar Manganian's mind was running along different lines. "He's just upset at the moment. He'll get over it."

"You think so, do you?" One eyebrow quivered and made a sudden leap up to the middle of his forehead. "I do not. Why is he not here now? Why did he run away as soon as the meeting ended? Why has he not returned—?" He held up a hand, cutting off any reply Tristram Quardon might have made.

"I will tell you why. Because he will not drink with me! Drink occupies a curious place in your English rituals, my friend. In perhaps no other corner of the earth are there so many customs and traditions centring around it. He will not drink with me because he is afraid it might be seen as a gesture of conciliation, perhaps even weakness. And so he has evaded joining us at the bar for drinks. He will not return—if he returns at all—until we are seated at the table. And watch him. Even then, he will only drink water."

"You're making too much of this, Ongar." Tristram Quardon protested, glancing at his watch. "I hadn't realized Mark had been gone so long. Perhaps he went down to his office and got caught by an incoming telephone call—"

"And perhaps he is making a telephone call. Even yet trying to find some way to block the merger. He is implacable, that man." The booming laugh rang out. "But so am I, my friend. So am I!"

"I'll have a word with him," Tristram said unconvincingly. It was patently obvious that he had noted Mark's long absence and had hoped that Ongar Manganian had been unaware of it. Or, at least, of the possible reason for it. "That's why I was looking for him just now. I thought you might have taken him aside for a word yourself."

"No, no, not I. He is the sort of man one speaks to only through lawyers. No—" Ongar Manganian looked around the kitchen, bright-eyed and bushy all over. "No, I am simply inspecting the troops." He smiled at Sidonie, but his eyes rested on Lexie. "They are not many, but they are choice."

Sidonie glowered at him from her far corner. Lexie simpered encouragingly, her hand creeping up to her top button.

I watched incredulously as she toyed with the button. He was not only grotesque, he was at least three times her age. She *wouldn't*, she *couldn't*. Not for *him*!

She did. The button sprang loose from its mooring and a few more inches of Lexie drifted into view.

She couldn't help it; it was born and bred into her. No matter what else he was, he was male and he was a multi-millionaire. The Sloane Ranger rides again!

Nevertheless, I made a grim mental note that we were all going to switch to bibbed aprons. *High*-bibbed aprons. I wouldn't like the clients to get the wrong idea about what was on the menu.

"Lunch is about ready, isn't it?" Tristram Quardon spoke directly to me, but sent a sideways frown to Lexie, reminding her. He might be her uncle and he might have arranged for her to join Executive Meal Service, but she was still in disgrace. The way she was behaving now would not get her off probation any faster.

With a pout, Lexie turned away and flounced over to speak to Sidonie, her back to the room.

"Ready whenever you are," I assured him.

"Mark probably slipped down to his office for a quick shave," Tristram said. "He's keeping everyone waiting." It was well known that Mark Avery had the sort of growth that required three or four shaves a day if he were not to look both shady and seedy. He was aware of this and hypersensitive about it, hence he was always slipping into the small bathroom attached to his office for a quick shave whenever he suspected the stubble was gaining on him again.

"Perhaps I ought to go and get him," Tristram said.

"I'll go," I said quickly. Mark Avery's office was two floors down and Tristram Quardon was not yet aware that the lifts weren't working. It was not so well known that Tristram Quardon had had a Pacemaker implanted about eighteen months ago. That was something else not particularly confidence-inspiring among the big-business types who sized up each other's health prospects over the port and wondered whether Old Smethers would make it through the next Annual General Meeting. Those of us who knew about it did what we could to ease his path.

"Tris—" One of the Directors appeared in the doorway. "Ongar—" He beckoned to them both. "Come and settle a little dispute, would you? We've just made a bet that—"

Tristram Quardon and Ongar Manganian followed him and their voices faded. I took a final look around before I went to call Mark Avery to lunch. I noticed that Lexie had shifted her position—presumably in case Ongar Manganian had taken another look as he left the room—and the arch of her back was distinctly provocative.

I decided that Sidonie and I would do the serving. There were too many opportunities for brushing and leaning during the course of serving a meal. I didn't want Tristram Quardon to begin wondering what Lexie might be getting up to in other Executive Dining-Rooms than his own. In point of fact, she had always behaved quite properly. But then Ongar Manganian was the first multi-millionaire who had ever come within striking distance.

You can't blame a girl for trying. But she wasn't going to try on my time. No, Lexie would sulk, but she would also stay in the kitchen this afternoon.

As it happened, I needn't have worried. Not about that. By the time the Directors came to their meal, no one had any appetite left . . . for anything.

Chapter

2

I tripped—literally tripped—over Edda Price as I entered Mark Avery's office. She was lying, in a neat diagonal line, just inside the door. Not unnaturally, I had entered the room looking around at eye level for its expected occupant. The door had opened easily and I had no reason to expect that a body would be stretched on the floor just a few feet beyond it. I advanced unsuspectingly into the room and nearly went sprawling.

I caught my balance just in time and looked down at the obstacle that had so nearly sent me flying. Edda lay face down and so motionless that I could not tell if she were breathing.

On top of the morning I had just had, it was too much. I closed my eyes and concentrated on deep breathing, fighting off the impulse to faint and thus opt out of any further responsibility in the matter. Joining her on the carpet would do no good at all. Deep breathing while counting slowly to one hundred might not help matters either, but at least it gave me the illusion that I was doing something about the situation. Or rather, that once I had reached my count and opened my eyes, I might be better able to cope with it.

I had reached thirty-three when a faint groan sounded at my feet. I opened my eyes and looked down.

"Where am I?" Edda Price had raised herself up on her elbows and was staring down at the carpet in bewilderment.

"You fainted." I helped her to turn over and sit up. "Are you all right now? Would you like a glass of water?"

"Water!" She looked around wildly and burst into tears. "Mark! Oh, Mark!" She lost all coherence as the sobs increased.

Water. I headed for Mark Avery's private bathroom. I wasn't sure whether to throw it over her or force her to drink it, but water was definitely indicated.

I stopped short in the doorway, swamped by a sense of *déjà vu*.

Mark Avery lay on his back, electric shaver still clutched in his hand. His eyes were wide open, staring at the ceiling. There was a blue tinge to his features which could not solely be accounted for by the stubble he had not had time to attack. I refused to think about the faint smell of something singed in the air.

"He's still there, isn't he?" Edda spoke immediately behind me, but I had not been conscious of footsteps. "It's not a nightmare?"

"It's a nightmare, all right," I said. "But it's real." I turned and the scene took on an even more nightmarish aspect.

Edda Price was still on the floor. Edda Price—the elegant Edda Price—had dragged herself across the carpet like something out of an old Lon Chaney silent film. She huddled beside the desk, tears rolling unheeded down her face, streaking it with mascara.

"Mark," she said again. "Oh, Mark! I found him. I tried to go for help, but I fainted. I was useless. And he died. Oh, Mark!"

"There was nothing you could do." I tried to comfort her. "If he was like that when you found him, there was nothing anyone could do. It was already too late."

I shouldn't have said that. With a moan, she lurched forward and began crawling towards the bathroom door to make sure that he *was* the way he was when she found him.

"No, please." I blocked her progress. "Come, sit here in the desk chair."

I tried to pull her upright, but she struggled and I gave up. She was in a state of shock and it was obviously too much to expect her to behave rationally. At the same time, I was quite shocked myself, particularly at her behaviour. I would never have believed that Edda Price could go to pieces so quickly or so thoroughly. I had always suspected her of having a secret passion for Tristram Quardon, but now I wondered whether it might not have been for Mark Avery.

Or was it simply that they had all worked together for so long that the business association had become transmuted into a form of family tie? Mark, Tristram and Edda had started out over a quarter of a century ago in a rickety little office in Long Acre and built Quardon International into a genuinely international company with its own office block in the City. When the first member of a tightly knit family died, the others were brought face to face with their own mortality.

"Someone will have to tell Tristram Quardon." The thought followed naturally.

"I can't—" Edda Price turned her stricken face to me. "The shock might kill him."

That was a possibility, but he would have to know sooner or later. The demise of so close a colleague was not something it would be possible to keep from him indefinitely. Particularly not in these circumstances.

"And a doctor—" My mind was beginning to function again. "We must call a doctor. Or perhaps an ambulance."

"But you said—" She had gained the chair, now she tried to struggle out of it, her face lighting with hope. "You mean, you're not sure? A doctor might be able to do something?"

"No. I'm sorry." I pushed her back gently. "It's just that one has to go through the motions. There has to be a doctor in the case of sudden death . . . accident . . ." The police had to be notified, as well, although I had a vague idea that would be taken care of automatically if we called for an ambulance reporting sudden death.

"It's all so terrible!" But she seemed to be pulling herself together. "I rang the Electricity Board to complain, but they denied there'd been a power cut in this area. I didn't believe them. I came down here to speak to Mark, let him deal with them. You know what they're like—they'll always pay more attention to a man. And I found him . . . like that." She closed her eyes briefly.

"Of course, there are things we must do." She stretched out a hand to the telephone and then seemed to give up on the idea—she wasn't that pulled together yet. She looked up at me pleadingly. "Send for Roddy."

I should have thought of that myself. Roddy Bletchley was Tristram Quardon's Personal Assistant. Some people said: heir apparent. Possibly and possibly not. All that was certain was that he functioned as troubleshooter and general dogsbody as well as personal assistant. But he was definitely one of the first who should be told.

After that, the whole mess could be left in his hands.

Automatically, I reached out towards the intercom, then remembered that it worked off the electric mains and so would be out of action. It would alert the switchboard if I tried to dial an inside number from here and curiosity might tempt one of the operators to listen—then the cat would be well and truly out of the bag.

"Look," I said, "we can't call from here. Why don't you slip upstairs quietly and have a word with him?" I wanted to get her out of the office before the second shock wave hit her. Once she began to think about it, she might crack wide open again.

"Wait a minute," I said, as she stood up in a daze of obedience. I couldn't let her walk out of here like that. I fumbled for a paper handkerchief from the box in the top right-hand desk drawer, but couldn't face going back into the bathroom.

"Spit," I ordered, as though to a child. Like a child, she obediently moistened a corner of the tissue and I scrubbed at the mascara streaks.

"All right." I inspected her without satisfaction. She would pass muster—but only just. And preferably in a very dim light. "Find Roddy and tell him to get down here. Don't talk to anyone else. If anyone tries to speak to you, tell them you have to see to the arrangements and go into the kitchen. Lexie and Sidonie are there. Don't tell them anything, either, but make them give you a brandy."

She gave a wisp of a nod and made her way carefully and a trifle unsteadily from the room.

Left alone, I closed my eyes and tried the deep breathing routine again, but it didn't work. As I had told Edda, there were motions that must be gone through. I was sure—I was as certain as I would ever be of anything in this life (or death)—but I had not tried to take Mark Avery's pulse. I had not held a mirror in front of his parted lips to see if the faintest trace of breath remained in his body. These things must be done.

I fought down the impulse to wait for Roddy and forced myself back into the bathroom.

The beard, hair and fingernails continue to grow until long after death. They're merely extruded protein with no life of their own; the condition of the host does not concern them so long as there are sufficient nutrients to sustain their growth.

I could not get that thought out of my mind and it seemed to me that Mark Avery's stubble was longer, thicker, than it had been when I first looked at him. The damned stuff had a life of its own, quite independent of poor Mark's. He had always claimed so and now the beard seemed intent upon proving it.

I averted my eyes and fumbled for his wrist. Nothing.

Perhaps I should have tried the Kiss of Life but I could not force myself to touch the cooling body again.

I lurched to my feet and went to the medicine cabinet, thinking that there might be a smaller mirror concealed inside. As I stood in front of the sink to swing back the mirrored door of the cabinet, I became aware of a strange sensation beneath my feet.

The carpet seemed . . . squidgy.

Already knowing what I must find, I looked down. The carpet was—or had been—sopping wet. It was still wet enough to give me an unsteady feeling, but the moisture was spreading outward into a wider patch of damp, being absorbed into the surrounding dry area. It looked as though someone had splashed a great deal of water on to the floor. Or perhaps the sink had overflowed. But the sink looked perfectly dry . . . drier than the carpet.

When I raised my eyes to the mirror, I did not recognize the pale haunted face staring back at me. The head was shaking faintly in a negative motion, denying the knowledge trying to fight its way upwards from my subconscious.

I stretched out my hand to steady myself against the wall. And then I saw the rest of it: the dark grey-blue scorch marks streaking outwards from the electricity socket into which Mark Avery's electric shaver was still plugged.

No wonder the electricity in the building had failed. Every fuse must have blown with the violence of that sudden deadly surge of power.

I pulled my hand away from the wall as though I had burned it. At that, I suppose we were lucky—everyone except Mark. A fire could easily have started and, with all the executives upstairs and the staff out at lunch, it could have gained a firm foothold and spread out to endanger, if not consume, most of the building before anyone discovered it.

I found that I could not stay in that room another moment. I backed out slowly, abandoning any thought of finding a mirror to hold in front of those bluish lips. With a jolt of electricity like that, resuscitation had to be started at once or it was useless. He had died when the clocks stopped. As I had told Edda, it had already been too late when she found him.

I couldn't remember whether the bathroom door had been open or closed when I went in. Not that it mattered, Edda Price had already been inside and would have opened the door if it had originally been closed. But nothing more should be touched; Roddy would realize that when he arrived.

I glanced at my watch. Just over an hour since all the electricity in the building had short-circuited, since Mark Avery had died.

Upstairs, the Directors would still be boozing merrily, although perhaps beginning to wonder just when luncheon would be served. It was lucky that no one else had decided to come looking for their missing Sales Director and Deputy Managing Director. How much longer could that luck be expected to hold?

Where was Roddy? Had Edda collapsed again on the way upstairs to find him?

"Oh-ho!" The voice from the doorway made me jump. "So this is where the chef is hiding." Ongar Manganian advanced into the office. "No wonder our meal has been delayed."

Where was Roddy? I felt a burst of irritation. Where the *hell* was Roddy? This was more than I could be expected to cope with. As Ongar Manganian had just pointed out, I was a chef. This was none of my business; I had my own business.

"I'm not hiding," I said coldly.

"No?" He frowned at me. "Then why aren't you? I have just had to walk down to this floor because the lifts are not working. On the way, I observed no lights in the corridors and that the electric clocks had stopped over an hour ago. Surely this means that your cooking apparatus is no longer serviceable and the meal is ruined. If I were the chef, I would go into hiding."

"The meal will be served as soon as—" I caught myself. "Shortly. If you will kindly return to the dining-room—"

"You were not this pale when I last saw you. Nor did your hands tremble." He surveyed me shrewdly. "Now, what has happened, I wonder?"

I remained mute. There was no need to speak, he was working it out for himself.

"You discover that your cooker is not working. You wish to make a complaint. But quietly, so that it may be fixed, if possible, in time to place the arranged meal before the Board of Directors on schedule, or so nearly on schedule that they will not notice anything has gone wrong."

In spite of myself, I felt my lips curve in a rueful smile. He was nearly right. It could so easily have happened that way. In which case, I would have been the one to discover Mark Avery and not Edda Price.

"The Directors, however, are celebrating our proposed merger in the bar. You cannot contact one of them quietly— the bar is too small. Everyone will overhear your problem and you do not want that. But there is one Director who feels he has no cause to celebrate. He has slipped away from the festivities, back to his own office. Perhaps to regain his composure, perhaps to begin regrouping his forces for a final attempt to reel the enemy. You know that he will be sympathetic to your plight and will help you—"

The sheer force of that overwhelming personality had been carrying me along with it, but now I became aware that I had begun shaking my head very slightly. It must have been noticeable, for he broke off abruptly and frowned at me. Still frowning, he looked around the office slowly.

"But where *is* Mark Avery?" With a swiftness surprising in so huge a bulk, he crossed to the bathroom and flung open the door. "Is he sulking in his tent?"

"Please—" I was too late to stop him from seeing what had happened, but I put my hand on his arm as he was about to enter for a closer look. "Don't go in there. There's nothing that can be done. We mustn't touch anything until—"

"Until the police arrive." He finished the sentence for me. "No, no. I see that you are right, little one. But what a terrible thing to have happened. I would not wish a fate like this on my worst enemy."

Nevertheless, an obscure satisfaction glinted deep in his eyes as he stared at his fallen foe. Mark Avery would do nothing more to block the merger.

"Christ! It's true!" Roddy had arrived at last. He was behind me, staring over my shoulder unbelievingly. "It's really true!"

"You thought, perhaps, that it was the sort of thing someone would tell you for a joke?" Ongar Manganian turned and looked at Roddy without favour.

"No . . . no, of course not . . . It's just—Christ!" He shook himself like a dog coming out of water and made an attempt to take charge of the situation.

"You'd better get upstairs," he told me. "Edda's breaking it to Tris. She'll need help."

He turned to Ongar Manganian. "I'm sorry, sir, but I'm afraid you shouldn't be here."

"Young man—" Ongar Manganian swept him with a contemptuous look. "I have not made my fortune by being in places where I was supposed to be."

Chapter
3

After that, of course, we might as well have been serving gall and wormwood. The Directors drank more than they ate, picking at the succulent salmon as though it were a heap of cinders. In hushed, unbelieving voices, they discussed the incredible fact that death had crept among them in the midst of their working day and made off with one of their number.

In his own office. That had shocked them more than anything. Business is the bulwark men build against mortality. They all knew the statistics on death after retirement. That was to be expected.

But in his own office, in the prime of life. If a man wasn't safe in his own office...

They finished the wine and went back to the whisky. The brandy wasn't neglected, either. Only the food. Anyone who had retained an appetite did not wish to seem disrespectful to the dead by indulging it. Drink, however, was looked upon as some sort of libation to the gods to be splashed about in propitiation for their temerity in surviving when one of their comrades had not.

It was also known as an Irish Wake.

* * *

It was a relief to clear up and leave. It was bliss to pull up in front of the large Notting Hill Gate detached that served Executive Meal Service as a headquarters and dive for the warmth and security of the big kitchen. Nick could unload the trays from the van later.

"You're back late." Mona looked up from stirring a large cauldron on the Aga cooker. "Everything all right?"

"Everything all wrong!" I hurled off my coat and fell into the comfort of the big welcoming rocking-chair Mona had insisted no kitchen should be without. "Couldn't be worse!"

Lexie and Sidonie rather spoiled the effect of this announcement by entering on a wave of giggles.

"Yes, it could," I corrected myself. "He might have died of ptomaine after gorging himself on the fish." A communal shudder vibrated through the kitchen. "Instead of which," I added quickly, "he died by accident before he ever got to the table."

"Who?" Mona advanced on me waving the ladle threateningly, drops of savoury soup flying from it. "Elucidate—immediately!"

I elucidated. Gretel crept from her post in the corner to listen wide-eyed.

Nick wasn't present; that meant he was still out scouring the highways and byways for the best buys of the day to bring back for us to build menus around. In practice, this meant Smithfield, Billingsgate and Nine Elms, but he often went farther afield, intercepting lorries of Common Market produce before they reached their assigned importer, inspecting the early crops in Green Belt farms to get the prime produce at the best prices. There was more than a bit of the highwayman in our Nick. It had served him well during his entrepreneurial days in an advertising agency and it was now working to our advantage as he threw his not-inconsiderable energies into both providing the raw materials for, and guiding the destinies of, Executive Meal Service.

"Thank heavens—" I was in the process of trying to describe Tristram Quardon's shock and distress when Mona interrupted. "Thank heavens, he hadn't eaten anything of ours."

"That's immaterial," I protested. "No one could confuse death by electrocution with death from ptomaine poisoning." Not even the solemn young policeman who had taken my statement before I had been allowed to leave.

"Oh yes they could—and don't you mistake it." Mona shook the ladle at me. "People like nothing better than to put two and two together and come up with twenty-five. There are always those who can make two facts equal one wild hypothesis. Especially," she added darkly, "in the media."

Gretel was blinking with the strain of trying to translate Mona's English into something that made sense. But there was no time to stop and try to explain to her that incomprehensibility was the point Mona was making.

"Anyway," I said, "we have an awful lot of salmon left over. It's all right, it never even went to the table. We served up in the kitchen. The Directors were in such a state they'd have hacked it to pieces and still not got a decent portion."

"I can imagine." She probably could. She had worked at director level herself before marrying Nick and retiring, as she had thought then, from the fray. "Well, we can do a nice salmon mousse for the cold table and anything still left over can go into the seafood vol-au-vents for tomorrow."

Gretel made a sound halfway between a gasp and a squawk and fled back to her corner. From the odour surrounding her, she had been cleaning shrimp for the canapés and vol-au-vents for tomorrow's reception at a new American bank. They had ordered a substantial finger buffet and specified individual cherry pies for dessert, since the whole thing was supposed to be a slightly belated celebration of George Washington's Birthday.

Mona raised her eyebrows and rolled her eyes upwards.

Gretel, I gathered, had been presenting a problem again. I nodded back at Mona sympathetically.

What can you do with the hopelessly cack-handed? Gretel was good-natured, energetic, enthusiastic, eager to learn and willing to throw herself into any task, however menial. Unfortunately, the resulting splash not only ruined the project in hand but meant that everyone in the vicinity had to stop whatever they were doing and help her to clean up. She had obviously been at it again this morning.

Since no one could be sure when Nick would return with his plunder, Lexie and Sidonie went outside and began unloading the van. Trying to appear casual, I got up and strolled around the kitchen, winding up in the corner where Gretel was working at a scrubbed pine side table.

It could have been worse. If often had been worse. This time, it was just a matter of the canapés losing out to the vol-au-vents. Immediately in front of Gretel was the waste bowl of pink and black threads—it was filling rapidly with more pink than black, but that was hardly worth mentioning. More serious was the fact that, of the other two bowls on the table, the one containing fragments of shrimp was nearly full whereas the bowl designated to hold whole shrimp was nearly empty.

Smiling at Gretel, but with an inward sigh, I opened another tin of shrimp and settled down to helping her.

"They are so small," she said defensively. "It is not easy to keep them in one piece."

"That's why we're doing seafood vol-au-vents at the same time." I tried to cheer her. "Nothing is ever wasted."

Perhaps it wasn't, but that wasn't Gretel's fault. I winced as another shrimp crumbled beneath her too-eager fingers. It was a pity. Gretel longed to do the really delicate work: glazing the aspic, piping mayonnaise scrolls, making confectionery roses, all the little finishing touches that added so much to a dish. The trouble was, if we let her near anything, it would be finished, all right.

The outer door crashed against the wall and Lexie and

Sidonie staggered into the kitchen laden with leftovers from the van. Lexie, carrying the serving platter with over half a salmon still to be seen beneath the plastic dome, just made it to the kitchen table where she deposited the platter with relief. Sidonie carried a large saucepan in each hand with boxes of mints and glacé fruits balanced on top.

"I've told you girls before," Mona scolded. "Don't try to unload everything all at once. It doesn't matter if you have to make several trips—and it's safer."

"Don't worry," Lexie giggled. "There are plenty more trips to make. This isn't nearly everything. If we'd known, we needn't have bothered to go there at all today, for all they've eaten." She and Sidonie turned and went out to the van again.

"They have such fun." Gretel watched them go, then turned mournful eyes to me, reminded afresh of another long-standing ambition. "When do you take me with you to cook the Boardrooms?"

"Some time," I said vaguely. *Some time between hell freezing over and the rivers running dry*. It was bad enough here where we could keep an eye on her, but what Gretel might do let loose in unfamiliar territory didn't bear thinking about.

I realized suddenly that, if she had been with us today, I should have seriously suspected her of being somehow to blame for Mark Avery's death. The manner of his accident had something of Gretel's clumsy incompetence about it. Imagine a man being killed by a freak accident with his own electric razor, which he must have used hundreds of times before! I was glad Gretel had been nowhere near the scene. It would have been only too easy to wonder secretly if she had been responsible in some way for that fatal wet patch on the carpet.

"You can do the shrimp flowers for tomorrow," I offered in apology for my unspoken thoughts. It ought to be all right. They were among our more foolproof canapés: a cracker spread with cream cheese, then one small whole shrimp placed in an upper corner for the flower and a long thin strip of green pepper placed beneath it like a stem, with another shorter sliver of green pepper midway up the first piece like another green sprig. It was simple but impressive, a plateful of them looked like a garden of spring blossoms. Surely even Gretel could manage that.

"Yes?" Her face lit up. She lurched to her feet, rocking the table. "I start now."

"No, no, tomorrow," I said, marvelling at how unerringly she had immediately leaped to do exactly the wrong thing. "You can't spread cream cheese on crackers and put them in the fridge for twenty-four hours," I reminded her. "They'll go soggy. They have to be the last things we make just before we leave for the reception."

"We?" Her face had been darkening, now it lit up again. "You are taking me with you?"

Over her head, I met Mona's eyes. There was no help there; she was trying not to laugh. I had boxed myself into a corner this time. Well, I supposed we had to start breaking Gretel in sooner or later. I only hoped the customers didn't break first.

"You'll have to be very careful," I surrendered. "Stay close to me and watch what the other girls do." There wasn't really anything she could do to ruin the reception, was there? And, even if she did, would anyone notice it? Americans weren't used to servants and tended to be touchingly grateful for any service rendered, if not overawed. If the rest of us could keep a straight face, any gaffe might be passed off as some quaint but obscure European tradition. The fact that Gretel had a "foreign" accent, as opposed to an English accent, would also be helpful. Whatever happened, we might just get away with it.

Lexie and Sidonie burst into the room again on another wave of hilarity. It was sheer reaction to the events of the day, of course. Sudden death took people that way sometimes, especially teenagers who had never encountered death before and who were not closely connected with the departed. Lexie might not find life so hilarious if it had been her uncle who had died rather than one of his business partners.

As it was, they were armoured in their youth and the unexpected brush with mortality had merely given an extra edge to life. Their own deaths were unthinkable, unbelievable, something that could never happen. Surely, long before they were old enough to begin to worry about it, medical science and the advances of technology would have rendered death obsolete. The fact that accidents could happen to anyone was not so much overlooked as ignored.

"That's it!" Lexie dumped a rack of dirty dishes beside the dishwasher. We had only washed up the china belonging to Quardon International when the electricity supply had been restored. We were so anxious to get out of there that we had brought our own dirty crockery back to be washed at home. "The last trip. The van is empty—we're finished."

"Good." Mona began loading the dishwasher. "Then you can start helping out here. I've hard-boiled the quails' eggs, Lexie, suppose you begin shelling them. Sidonie can start mixing the savoury sausagemeat to wrap around them. We're doing miniature Scotch eggs for the buffet." She shrugged and we knew what she meant. The small individual Scotch eggs would be far more expensive than the regular ones made with hens' eggs, but they were also far more impressive. The American bank was determined to impress their guests and it was to be a no-expense-spared occasion. Not that we were complaining. We would make a nice profit on it, although not half as nice as the wine merchant would.

"Scotch eggs!" Lexie giggled wildly. "Most Americans have never seen them and don't know what to do with them." She giggled again. "Did I ever tell you about that time in New York—?" She was overcome by laughter.

We all waited expectantly. We had heard quite a bit about Lexie's time in New York—although none of it from her. The newspapers had been full of it when she eloped to New

York with an early boy-friend. No marriage ever took place and the newspapers had been far more excited about it than Lady Pamela, Lexie's mother, who had simply shrugged her shoulders and said, "They'll come home when their money runs out." Which, of course, was exactly what had happened, although the money might have lasted a bit longer if they hadn't splashed it about cutting a swathe through the most expensive places in New York.

The media excitement had died down after her return, although she was still good for a paragraph or two in the gossip columns. But that sort of thing didn't ruin a girl's marriage chances any more. Not in ordinary circles. And not even the most insanely ambitious mother could have thought of Lexie as regal marriage material. Probably not even ducal. A nice merchant banker, however, or Something in the City. . . now that was more realistic for Lady Pamela to pin her hopes on.

But after a year or so, during which there had been a number of romances—none of them developing into anything permanent—Lexie had been persuaded to make a gesture towards a career. She had always been interested in cooking. Indeed, her only souvenirs from her fling in New York had been a pile of American cookbooks and the conviction that she was an expert on American affairs. Since Executive Meal Service was already working for Quardon International, Tristram Quardon had unhesitatingly pulled the right string on behalf of his late brother's only child and Alexia Quardon was now working/studying with us. Almost automatically, Sidonie, her closest friend and some sort of distant cousin, had come along with her as, I gathered, she had tagged along since childhood on anything Lexie did. Except, of course, her wildest exploits, like the New York elopement.

It had worked out better than any of us had any right to expect. Both girls were genuinely enthusiastic about cooking, the fees paid for their tuition went a long way towards keeping Executive Meal Service solvent, and two willing assistants meant that we did not need to hire temporary catering staff for our bigger contracts like tomorrow's reception. Even on the smaller assignments, it meant that Mona no longer had to go out with me to help serve luncheons and could remain behind in the kitchen cooking towards the next meal, answering telephone calls, typing invoices and otherwise concentrating on firming up the business we already had and canvassing new clients. We were very close to the turning-point, to the place where just getting by gave way to making a positive profit and led on to the road to success. Every little bit helped. Even Gretel.

"Please—" Gretel said, as Lexie fought to overcome her hysterical laughter. "The Scotch eggs. You are going to tell us? Yes?"

"Yes, tell us," Mona encouraged. While this had been going on, she had been tossing equal parts of olive oil, soy sauce and cooking sherry into a large bowl. Now she added appropriate amounts of garlic and dry mustard and stirred it all vigorously before going to prepare the chicken livers. "We can all use a laugh."

"My God—we can!" I echoed fervently. In the warm sheltering kitchen, buttressed by laughter and friendship, the horror of the day was beginning to recede. I watched Mona pull a thawed chicken liver from the defrosting mass and cut away the bits of clinging fat and membrane. She sliced the remaining liver into bite-sized pieces and tossed them into the marinade where they would remain overnight.

"Yes, well—" Lexie took a deep breath and pulled herself together. "We were sitting around in a cocktail bar one night—a whole crowd of us drinking. And, as usual, there was nothing to eat but salty peanuts and crisps. I wanted something to eat, but not a full meal. But you can't get any food in cocktail bars, you have to go into the dining-room if they're part of a restaurant, or else leave and go somewhere else. Even then, you have to have a whole meal."

"They don't have the law we have here that says any

place that sells drinks also has to sell food.'' Mona gave a faint sigh, perhaps for the days when she and Nick went on those expense account trips to New York and Chicago. ''They aren't obliged to provide any sort of snacks.''

''And they don't,'' Lexie said. ''I started complaining about it and then I went on to reminiscing about our English pubs and all the lovely things you could get: Ploughman's lunch, enormous hot sausages, shepherd's pie, Scotch eggs, the lot. Oh, I had a real old fit of nostalgia, I can tell you. Not only that,'' she added, not without a touch of pride, ''I carried all the rest of them along with me—and most of them had never even seen a real English pub. But, by the time I was done, they were all sighing.''

I could well believe it. Even now, we were all hanging on her words. Lexie could carry anyone along with her. Even Sidonie, who must have heard the story before.

''Well, naturally—'' Lexie gave a dismissive shrug—''I'd forgotten about it by next day. And I never expected anyone else to remember. Then we went to dinner at a friend's—'' Every now and again, Lexie let slip a ''we,'' the only indication she ever gave that she had not been on her own in New York.

''And I found—'' she was back on form—''that she'd tried to cook a real English meal for me because she thought I was getting homesick. The only trouble was—'' she giggled again—''I must have left something out when I was telling her about Scotch eggs, or she misunderstood completely. You should have seen them! Well, no—'' she corrected herself—''they *looked* all right. It was when we cut into them, we discovered what she'd done.

''She'd wrapped the sausagemeat around raw eggs and then deep-fried them until the meat was cooked. At first, we couldn't get the knife through because of the shell, then it sort of *splashed* through. You never saw such a mess in your life!''

''Oh, I don't believe it!'' Gretel was whooping with

delight at the idea of someone worse in the kitchen than she was. "Oh, that is so funny! Did it really happen?"

It was never possible to know whether Lexie's stories were actually true, but she told an awfully good story. We were all laughing and relaxed.

"It's true," Lexie maintained. "Honestly, it is. Then I had to explain that you were supposed to hard-boil the egg first and take the shell off. But she should have known. Who could ever imagine doing a Scotch egg that way?"

A car horn sounded abruptly outside the house and Lexie glanced at her watch. "Oh heavens, that's Humpty already! He said he'd pick me up, but I didn't expect him so soon—" She looked at us apologetically, pleadingly. "And there's still so much to do."

"He's not all that early," I said. "We're running late. Unavoidable circumstances today. You can run along now, but try to be here early tomorrow. There's going to be a lot of work."

"I will, I promise." She was halfway out the door when she hesitated, as though caught by a sudden thought. "I know Mona hates the idea," she said, "but, honestly, you ought to get a microwave oven. They're all over New York—and they're so fast. We could get everything done in a fraction of the time."

"And then you need a regular oven anyway," Mona countered, "to brown everything. It only doubles the work."

"Oh, but—" Lexie began. The horn sounded again. She pouted. "He's in a bad mood tonight." She waved. "See you in the morning." She was gone.

"If the rest of you would like to leave now—" I looked at Sidonie and Gretel.

"I'm in no hurry," Sidonie said, a trifle grimly. She shared a flat with Lexie, but it was obvious that she wasn't included in Lexie's plans for this evening.

"Nor I," Gretel said sunnily. "There! The shrimps are finished. What do we do now?"

"I hate to say this, but—the dishes." I gestured towards

the dishwasher and the remaining jumble of dirty crockery they had carried in from the van. It was an empty gesture, most of them would have to be washed by hand; Mona had filled the machine with the easy load.

Two heavy sighs answered me, but I hardened my heart. The first rule every cook learns is: the person who makes the meal isn't the one who does the dishes. Not if there's anyone else within a two-mile radius who can be conned into doing them. It's a question of self-preservation, which is, of course, the first law of Nature.

Speaking of which, I heard the sound of a car pulling into the carriageway and stopping at the side of the house. Nick was back.

Chapter
4

When Nick bounded into the kitchen a moment later, he was looking too triumphant for comfort. *Our* comfort, that is. His eyes were just a little too bright and his smile too charming. There was just a trace of uncertainty in his manner as he looked around the kitchen, rubbed his hands together and said, "Ah, it's good to be home."

"Is it?" Mona eyed him suspiciously. "In that case, why didn't you get here a lot earlier?"

"Ah—" He raised one hand in a defensive gesture, warding off criticism. "I'll bet you're wondering where I've been all day. You'd never guess. Not in a thousand years."

"Try me," Mona said flatly. "You've been drinking with the boys from the Agency."

"Only in passing." He was wounded. "On the way back, after a hard day tracking down a sensational bargain for you. It's tied to the top of the car—that's why I had to wait until the rush hour was over. I couldn't drive through traffic like that. Wait until you see it! Come and give me a hand getting it into the house."

Mesmerized, we followed him through the back door and out into the yard, prepared to unload bushels of sprouts, a ton of potatoes, or whatever he had picked up at bargain prices. Then Mona gasped as we saw it.

It sprawled like some giant prehistoric monster, legs in air, all the way across the roof of the shooting brake and jutted out over the sides.

"Isn't it a beauty?" Nick demanded, beginning to unlash ropes. "Did you ever see anything like it?"

"No," Mona said faintly. "What is it?" Since it was obviously a table, she was playing for time with the question. Time to gather her wits about her and decide how best to deal with the situation. Not that she had much choice, Nick had presented us with a *fait accompli*.

"Genuine rosewood," he misunderstood cheerfully. "There are three leaves for it inside. One of them's a bit warped, but the boys in the Road ought to be able to give us a hand with that." He disappeared around to the other side of the shooting brake to tackle some more knots.

"Leaves..." Mona murmured weakly. We looked up at the enormous table. "It's got three leaves."

"It is magnificent," Gretel approved. "You must be able to seat forty around it. You will be able to hold banquets."

"Banquets..." Mona echoed. She raised her voice in a cry of anguish. "Nick!"

"All right," he shouted. "I'm going to slide it off the roof, blanket and all. Stand by to catch it. Lower it to the ground gently and right side up. As soon as it's moving, I'll come round to help you."

We leaped forward as the table quivered and began to tilt. It slid smoothly and more quickly than we had been prepared for, the blanket protecting its surface accelerated its progress.

My first thought was that I'd rather be unloading a ton of potatoes. Certainly, the table seemed to weigh a ton—and it was all in one piece. Suddenly, we were fighting to prevent it crashing to the ground.

"All right." Nick arrived to reinforce us. While we tried to hold the table steady against the side of the shooting brake, he turned it so that the legs were where they belonged and suddenly it was standing upright.

"Fine," Nick said. "Now let's get it into the house. Gretel, Sidonie, there are three chairs inside the brake with the leaves. One upright and two carvers. Matching. Three trips ought to do it."

Nick, Mona and I wrestled the table sideways through the door and into the kitchen. It took up most of the room. Sidonie and Gretel staggered in behind us with the two carvers.

"Whew!" Sidonie set down her chair and collapsed into it. She propped her elbows on the arms of the chair and looked down over it approvingly. "Lovely bit of stuff, this."

"Rosewood. The original match to the table, I'd say." Nick shook his head. "Too bad we couldn't get the full set, but I imagine it got broken up over the years. They probably survived because they doubled as armchairs. Only one dining chair, though. Still, we can find something close enough in the Road and we wouldn't have been able to afford it if it had been complete."

"What—?" Mona asked through clenched teeth. "What are we going to do with it? Where are we going to put it?"

"The dining-room, of course." Nick looked surprised. "It's empty. High time we began furnishing it."

"The table is far too big for it," Mona said.

"Nonsense. It's just the right size. It's an enormous room. We'll still have space for a sideboard, a couple of wine coolers, the rest of the chairs—when we find them—"

"I mean, it's too big for *us*," Mona said.

"Ah! Well—" There was a delicate silence.

"Come on, Gretel." Sensitive to atmosphere, Sidonie got to her feet. "Let's go and bring in the rest of the things . . ."

"Suppose we carry it through to the dining-room," Nick coaxed. "Then we can see how it looks." He signalled to me and I took my station at the end of the table. Mona stood back and watched us grimly as we managed to shove it out of the kitchen and down the hallway.

"There we are." Nick positioned the table in the centre of the great empty room. "Could have been custom-made for this dining-room."

I had to agree. Large as the table was, there was still plenty of space. The dining-room was in keeping with the rest of the house, a late-Victorian family dwelling, designed in the days when "family" was understood to mean husband, wife, ten children, grandparents, several indigent relatives and a dozen or so live-in servants to accommodate them all. Not surprisingly, it had stood empty for decades until Nick, in the first flush of being appointed Accounts Director at the advertising agency where he worked, had bought it for rather more than a song and a staggering mortgage. It fitted in with his grandiose ideas of a suitable home for a rising young executive. Once it had been properly done up and furnished, that is.

"Quick—help me to get this off." Nick began tearing at the string securing the tattered blanket to the table top. "Before she gets here." We could hear Mona's footsteps coming slowly down the hallway.

I attacked the string on my side of the table. The knots resisted my efforts. Nick had tied them to stay tied and protect his precious rosewood surface.

"Damn!" I felt a fingernail give, while the knots still held.

"Here—let me." Nick had untied his side; he came round and began working at the knots with an anxiety bordering on desperation. I knew he wanted Mona to see the full beauty of the table as she came into the room.

"There—" The last stubborn knot gave way and he pulled at the blanket, unveiling the table.

"Oh, Nick! It *is* lovely." I knew Mona stood in the doorway, but all my attention was for the table. It was beautifully patterned, glowing with the patina of a tenderly polished and cherished piece of furniture. "Where did you find it?"

"Sometimes you strike it lucky at these country auctions," he said. "I was doubly lucky. There was a heavy fog down there and I think some of the dealers who'd ordinarily have bid it out of sight must have got lost or discouraged trying to find the place."

"How much?" Mona was not going to be sidetracked by minor considerations.

"We'll earn it back in no time," Nick said. "With this, we can cater for private parties right here in the house. Just think, no more chasing around with containers, trying to keep food hot or cold, no more struggling in strange kitchens—"

"In the house," Mona said flatly. The words hung in the air accusingly.

"We'll still be out a lot," I said quickly. "There won't be all that many people who'll want to trail away over here for their meal. And I can't see our business clients holding their Board meetings here just to be convenient to the kitchen."

"Oh, not the City trade," Nick said. "We'll just have to continue to cope with that. I was thinking of new business. People who might want to discuss confidential business over a meal and don't want to go to restaurants where they might be overheard. People who want to entertain clients at some place exclusive but undiscovered. Testamonial dinners to departing directors from their colleagues. Oh, we'll find plenty of new business, don't worry. Of course, at first, they'll have to bring their own wines with them—until we can get a liquor licence. But I don't suppose they'll find that any great strain—and it will work out cheaper for them—"

His enthusiasm was mounting. He did not seem to notice that he had lost Mona.

"Liquor licence," Mona said. "You mean you're planning to turn our home into a restaurant?"

"More of a private dining club, actually," Nick said. "Very private. Reservations only. We pick and choose."

Sidonie and Gretel had carried in the last table leaves. They looked from Mona to Nick and then glanced at each other. With one accord, they leaned the leaves against the wall in a corner and moved together.

"I'm afraid we'll have to go now." Sidonie acted as spokesman. "We'll be here early in the morning. Nine o'clock?"

"Good!" Mona said absently. She probably hadn't heard a word, but the fact that they were leaving had got through to her.

"I say good night then." Gretel continued to try to observe the amenities, but Sidonie caught her arm and pulled her through the doorway. We could hear their footsteps hurrying down the hallway.

"Good night," Nick called after them.

"I ought to get back to my quarters," I said cravenly. "It's going to be a busy day tomorrow—"

"No hurry." Nick shot me a betrayed look. "Why don't we go back to the kitchen and have a drink?"

"—and it's been quite a day today," I finished firmly. "It's been a terrible day. Mona will fill you in on it. I just want to go off and collapse. Alone."

It was the best I could do towards throwing him a lifeline. He was going to have to face Mona by himself sooner or later. Perhaps by the time she had finished explaining—if he could persuade her to explain—what had happened at Quardon International, some of her anger might have been deflected.

"Wait a minute—" Nick began. But I walked out of the room as though I hadn't heard him. I didn't dare do otherwise.

The trouble was that, while I sympathized with Mona, I was on Nick's side. And not just because I was his sister. His idea was good and a logical progression along the path we were travelling. Furthermore, we needed the extra money.

My heart went out to Mona because I could also understand her feelings. The house had been bought to serve as their home. Of course, she wanted to keep it for themselves. It was bad enough that I had already encroached on it. But that was unavoidable—if they wanted to keep it at all.

No one could have forseen the way the economic climate had changed over the past few years: the rising and falling pound, the shrinking markets, the tightening belts, the closures, the redundancies, the frantic scrabbling to stay in one's accustomed position. Inevitably, advertising had been one of the worst-hit areas; the first thing a tightly pressed company thought of economizing on. In Nick's agency, the accounts had fallen away or shrunk to a size which made an overall Accounts Director an unnecessary luxury. The regular account executives could easily handle what business there was.

Nick had held out until the Golden Handshake, although "it was more like tin," was the way he had phrased it. Not enough to pay off the mortgage, let alone keep him in the manner to which he had become accustomed. Nor was anything better in the offing anywhere. There were too many redundant advertising executives chasing too few openings. The smart ones veered off into different fields.

Nick had looked around for a growth industry requiring minimal investment but promising maximum returns. Inevitably, his eye had fallen on me.

I had been back in England for about a year after a stint in Brussels working as a secretary for Common Market Eurocrats. It was the usual dreary story, it bored even me by this time: high hopes, growing disillusionment, a broken romance and the realization that I was getting nowhere and not likely to improve on the situation in an overpriced, overrated job which took more of my time and energy than it was worth.

Back in England, I couldn't seem to settle to anything that appealed to me. I worked as a temp for a while but, despite constant offers to join the permanent staff, I realized that any of the jobs offered would bore me rigid before I'd even learned the name of the upper hierarchy.

I fell into it almost by accident. Prowling the street markets in an effort to offset the dreariness of my tiny room in a shared flat by searching out "personal touches" to make it "my own," I began to notice the situation of the stallholders. Stuck behind their counters throughout an end- less Saturday, dependent upon friends and fellow stallholders to run errands and/or spell them while they attended to necessities, they were an entire captive market in themselves.

I had always enjoyed cooking and, like Lexie with her American recipes and cookbooks featuring 1001 ways with hamburgers, my main souvenirs from my foreign experi- ences were sheaves of simple but exotic recipes. I had nothing much to lose and during one week when my flatmates were out at work, I took over the communal kitchen and produced a few crocks of patés and several Quiches Lorraines. On the Saturday, it was then a simple matter buying, slicing and buttering several loaves of French bread, loading it all into my little Citröen and setting out to see how I fared.

I was sold out before I was halfway down Portobello Road and realized I was on to a winner.

Before long, I had traded in the Citröen for the present- day small blue van, invested in a portable coffee urn and added several more street markets to my rounds. I made a welcome change from the travelling hamburger and hot dog vans and even the ice-cream man. It wasn't much longer before I realized that I could do with some help and Mona began coming along with me occasionally. Gradually, I realized that I could also do with more room, a bigger kitchen and some financial backing in order to branch out and perhaps explore different markets.

It was at this point that Nick and I settled down for a long serious talk.

The result was that we formed an alliance—or, perhaps, simply reinforced the alliance we had had since childhood. Nick turned in his sports car for the shooting brake and began to learn the ins and outs of bulk buying. Mona was another cooking fiend and the kitchen was equipped with the original Aga, still going strong after an overhaul when they moved in. Their freezer compartment incorporated in the refrigerator was too small, so we had invested in a second-hand deep-freeze unit and decided we had the basic equipment necessary.

I gave up my room in the shared flat and moved into the attic flat which had belonged to the original housekeeper and was, therefore, already set up with bedroom, sitting-room, bathroom and tiny kitchenette and in fairly good order—unlike the rest of the house. All I had needed to do was to paint and furnish it and my friends in the street markets had helped me with that. I meticulously paid Mona and Nick the rent I had been paying in the other flat and I knew that it was more of a help than they preferred to admit.

It was not Mona's fault that I sometimes felt like a cuckoo in the nest.

I sympathized, even though I thought it was unreasonable, if not totally unrealistic, of her to expect to have a house of that size just for themselves. Especially when Nick no longer had the wherewithal to keep it going without help.

Naturally, every woman wanted a home of her own. So did I. But a place of this size would be better run as a restaurant or hotel. It was surprising that it had not been bought by a property speculator and cut up into flats or let out as bedsitters.

Even though I occupied the top story, Mona didn't know how lucky she was. Perhaps Nick could persuade her of that. I was too tired to worry about it tonight.

I had a hot bath and went to bed. I fell into an uneasy sleep teeming with nightmares of being chased across a wet and slippery rosewood table the size of a football field, pursued by a buzzing electric razor.

Chapter
5

In the morning, it was all hands to the pump.

Nick was shelling almonds when I walked into the kitchen and Mona was making piecrust for the cherry tarts. I helped myself to a cup of coffee from the pot keeping hot at the back of the stove and noted with approval that a big kettle of thick beef stew was simmering away towards lunch-time. It was all very well tasting and nibbling away as one worked, but it was no substitute for a proper lunch. The bits and pieces didn't really fill you up and you soon got bored with nibbling away at the goodies. Apart from which, they were destined for the reception this evening and it would be horrible to run short.

"Something good and hearty, I thought," Mona said, seeing the direction of my gaze. "Fill up the little tummies and help keep the little fingers out of the till."

"Quite right," I said. We had been working with food for so long that the novelty had worn off, but the girls were still new to it and considered nibbling part of the perks. They had not yet assimilated the basic fact that, in our line of business, food represented money—often quite a sizeable investment. Mona wasn't entirely joking when she talked about keeping little fingers out of the till.

I was delighted to see that Mona was in a joking mood. It meant last night's squall had blown over and we could all work in harmony again. A state much to be desired when six people were sharing the same kitchen and working towards a deadline.

No matter how excellent your basic materials, food still has to be prepared and presented with loving care. I wouldn't go so far as believing old wives' tales about milk curdling if the cook gave it a sour look, but there is no doubt that a pleasant atmosphere added a great deal to the meal long before it was time to serve it. I had seen restaurant kitchens where this was not the general rule, of course—and it was just as well the public never had any idea of what went on in them.

"Acting on the same theory," Nick said, "I thought I'd get these out of the way before the little darlings arrived. They're altogether too tempting." He had a large bowl full of shelled almonds now and he poured them into a large strainer and suspended it in a pan of boiling water, shaking it gently for a few seconds before lifting it out again. Then he began pinching the skins off the blanched almonds. A small pan of melted butter was already nestled on the corner of the stove. Brushed with the melted butter and popped into the oven on a buttered baking tray until they were golden and then salted and cooled, he would produce expert salted almonds at a fraction of the cost of those bought ready-made in tins. He was right, they were altogether too tempting to leave around when the girls arrived.

"There's a side of smoked salmon in the larder," Mona told me. "I think it would be best if you sliced that now. We'll let one of the girls butter the brown bread and you can assemble the sandwiches later. That will cut down on the more expensive depredations."

"Fine." I drained my coffee and went into the huge larder

opening off the kitchen. It was a sight to delight the heart of the original Victorian housewife who had first lived here.

Strings of onions and bags of drying herbs hung from hooks in rafters embedded in the ceiling, as did several large smoked hams and strings of smoked sausages. Huge white pottery crocks of marinating chicken livers and drumsticks were ranged along the lower shelves waiting to be transferred to baking pans and the oven.

On the next row of shelves, baked pie cases and vol-au-vent shells waited to be filled with sweet or savoury mixtures and popped into a hot oven. Behind them were ranged jars and tins of luxury items: truffles, olives, pimentoes, maraschino cherries, pickled pearl onions, green peppercorns, foie gras, an assortment of honey, preserves, varieties of olive oil, and all sorts of expensive impulse buys purchased when we were feeling flush and hoarded against the day when they might be just what we needed for some exotic dish.

There was even a joke in (literally) bad taste: a tin of Mexican chocolate-covered ants, donated by Nick on a day when he had returned from an exceedingly liquid lunch with ex-colleagues. Mona and I had vowed that some day we would make him eat them all by himself.

The higher shelves were filled with spices, from allspice and basil through to saffron. In the cupboards beneath the shelves lurked the staples: bags of short and long grain rice, macaroni and pasta shapes, barley, lentils, red kidney beans, dried split peas, whole grain flour, maize, cracked wheat flour, even—whisper it not in the more rarified establishments—enriched white flour.

It occurred to me that I really ought to check with Nick at some point to make sure that our insurance cover took all these comestibles into consideration. They really did constitute a large outlay of capital and, at the current rate of inflation, their replacement value would be considerable.

I picked up the polythene-shrouded slab of smoked salmon

and carried it back into the kitchen. I set it down at the far end of the table from Mona and reached absently for a knife.

"Not that one!" Mona said sharply. "That's the one I'm saving to cut Nick's throat with!"

"Ooops, sorry." There had been an underlying venom in that joke. Nick wasn't completely forgiven yet; no wonder he was helping out so enthusiastically. "I'm a million miles away."

"Your knives are over there—" Mona gestured towards the side table. "You'd better take what you want and put the rest away before the girls arrive."

"I'll do that." Every good cook has her own set of knives; she carries them from job to job; they are as personal as a toothbrush and no one else is allowed to use them. I had nearly committed a cardinal sin by picking up one of Mona's knives. I must pay more attention, my knives had black handles and Mona's had brown handles, so dark a brown they were nearly black, but I was expected to know the difference. Of course, if I had actually started to use it, I'd have noticed instantly that it wasn't mine.

Since the arrival of our apprentices, we had invested in a communal set of knives for them to use. They were good adequate knives and would do for them to train with. Already they were acquiring a dull and battered look, but that didn't matter. Nick could sharpen them up well enough and the girls were learning to take better care of their equipment. Already Gretel was saving up to buy a set of knives of her own. What Gretel might do with a brand new set of razor-sharp knives didn't bear thinking about, but perhaps she would be more expert by the time she actually acquired them.

I selected the knife for the smoked salmon and locked the others away.

Nick winked at me as he shoved the baking tray full of almonds into the oven. "That's done," he said. "Why don't we all take a coffee break now?"

"Because you have to peel the potatoes so that the girls

can make crisps." Mona was not letting him off easily. "They can nibble at those, if they want to. It will keep them out of worse mischief."

"And what about me?" he grumbled. "Why don't we buy a mechanical potato peeler? We could use one."

"Because we've got to buy Regency-stripe wallpaper and some paint and do up the dining-room now that you've decided we're going to use that. *And* we're going to do up the hallway properly, as well."

So that was how he had got round her. Having bought the house originally, they had had little money left to begin making any improvements. They had painted the outside and then intended to do up the rooms they would most use, planning to work their way through the house. Most fortunately, Mona had insisted that the kitchen take priority. They had hardly begun on their living-room and bedroom when the writing began to appear on the walls of Nick's office.

All further renovations had been prudently suspended. It was the sensible thing to do. At the same time, one couldn't blame Mona if it rankled a bit. Here she was, rattling around in an enormous ark of a house, which looked imposing on the outside, but only had two-and-a-half livable rooms inside. The half was the large drawing-room on the first floor overlooking the front garden and magnolia tree. In fact, it was more like one-third, since there was only a long sofa and coffee table huddled in front of the fireplace and the rest of the room was bare, although freshly wallpapered and painted just before the work had to stop.

I was well aware that the fact that I had done some renovating on my attic flat was the main reason Mona had welcomed me into her home without too much hesitation. Sooner or later, I would want to move out into a larger flat or house of my own and those rooms would revert to Mona and would need only minimum attention to dilapidations to raise them to satisfactory standard again. It didn't always keep me from feeling that I was there on sufferance, though.

"We'll go shopping tomorrow," Nick promised. They

must have had quite a session after I left last night, he was not usually so prompt to redeem his promises—especially where spending money was concerned. Not that he could be blamed for that. Although the situation was gradually improving, we hadn't had a great deal of money to throw around.

"Mind your almonds," Mona warned. "They don't take long."

"I'll just give them a shake." Nick swung open the oven door and did so. "Another couple of minutes."

"Too late." I heard a clatter at the back door. "Here come the locusts."

Nick moved away from the oven hurriedly, but it was only Gretel.

Gretel was another legacy from my Common Market days. Her father had been one of the friends with whom I had kept in contact. When he had heard that I had taken on Lexie and Sidonie as student/apprentices, he had immediately written to enroll his elder daughter. She wanted to try her wings and he did not like the idea of her going to some strange family as an *au pair*. But, as a cookery student, watched over by a friend, that was the perfect solution. The cheque he enclosed had made it a hard offer to refuse and Gretel had duly arrived and seemed to be happy, although impossible in the kitchen.

"Just in time," Nick greeted her. "You can come and help me peel potatoes."

"No, she can't," Mona said. "I want her to get some practice on the mandoline. Give her the potatoes as you peel them and she'll do the crisps."

"Oh yes!" Gretel beamed. "I am so glad I am first today. I get the peach job."

"Plum," Nick corrected with a groan. Peeling the potatoes for her was going to be a major chore.

She would have been given the mandoline anyway. As Mona said, she needed practice. Not that, in Gretel's case, practice was likely to make perfect, but it might reduce her clumsiness a bit. In any case, potatoes were cheap and plentiful just now and we could toss her failures into the stew.

"Do you know—" Gretel accepted a peeled potato from Nick and ground it against the mandoline—"I do not—"

"Gently dear," Mona said. "You don't need to saw at it."

"Yes." Gretel modified her stroke. "I do not think Sidonie is happy."

"Everyone can't be happy all the time." Nick might not have been aiming his comment solely at Gretel. He tossed another peeled potato into the bowl beside her.

"No," Gretel frowned. "But she came back to my flat last night and she was in a very strange mood. Not happy."

"She'd had a hectic day," I said. "It was rather awful at Quardon. I shouldn't think anyone was happy yesterday."

"It was not that," Gretel said. "I fixed us a meal and she was very quiet. I think something was bothering her."

If she'd eaten the meal, it was probably nothing that a little bicarbonate of soda couldn't take care of.

"Nick—the almonds," Mona said quickly, before he could voice the thought in all our minds.

"What did you give her?" I asked curiously.

"Something simple, I plan, after such a day. I do soup and nice little sandwiches." Gretel paused thoughtfully in her labours. "But they were not so nice. Is a very confusing language, English. I want nice sandwiches like you make with the meat paste and the fish paste for tea. But I want something a little different. The soup is too bland, so I make sandwiches with curry paste. It was not the same thing at all. Sidonie explained to me after we throw them away. She says there is even a paste for artificial jewels." Gretel sighed deeply. "This, I do not understand."

Nick managed to keep a straight face until his back was turned. He removed the tray of almonds, but Gretel was too absorbed to notice. The circles of potato had not yet achieved uniform thickness and often fell away from her mandolin in chunks and incomplete circles.

"Straight through to the larder, Nick," Mona directed. "Salt them there and leave them to cool. I hear the others coming."

"Mmm—something smells good!" Lexie burst into the kitchen, followed closely by Sidonie.

"Everything smells good," Mona corrected. "Or soon will do. Into your aprons, quickly! This is our busy day."

"Panic stations!" Lexie giggled. "Which one is mine?"

"I want you on the blender," Mona said. "They've ordered dips. We'll give them bowls of onion, devilled ham and sherried crabmeat dip. That ought to keep them happy. Gretel is making the crisps for the dips."

"Perhaps we ought to give them crackers, too," Sidonie said, doubtfully eyeing Gretel's struggles with the mandoline. Her fingers twitched. She was obviously longing to take the mandoline away from Gretel and slice the potatoes herself. Her crisps would be wafer-thin and perfect. But Gretel had to learn and she was paying for her course, too.

"It doesn't matter." Lexie shook tabasco sauce into the first blender bowl with lavish abandon. "Americans don't pay that much attention. Just make the dip spicy enough and you can give them bits of old horseblanket to dip into it and they won't know the difference."

"We'll stick with crisps," Mona said. "And perhaps cheese straws," she conceded to Sidonie. "But watch that tabasco—there's a difference between making it spicy and burning their palates out."

"Don't worry." Lexie poured in more sour cream and splashed in cooking sherry. "They'll never notice. They'll eat anything—especially the men. One of the worst things I ever tasted was some chocolates made to what they claimed was an Old American recipe. They had *wintergreen* filling!" She grimaced. "It was like eating chocolate-covered toothpaste."

"Sidonie—" Mona distracted the girl's attention: she still

seemed perilously close to snatching the mandoline from Gretel and doing the job properly herself. "Sidonie, perhaps you'd do the cheese straws. You'll find some puff pastry on the shelf in the butler's pantry. I took it out of the deep-freeze hours ago, so it should be defrosted by now. And bring in the crabmeat for Lexie, would you, please?"

The butler's pantry was next door to the larder, a long narrow room, again with plenty of shelves—well, he had to have somewhere to stack the silver plate, didn't he? Those were the days. We found it ideal for the deep-freeze locker. There was also a lock on the door, which we never used but always felt that it might be useful some day—just in case we were ever able to afford any of those silver serving dishes.

Sidonie returned and silently handed the packet of crabmeat to Lexie, then settled to rolling out pastry for the cheese straws at the large Victorian washstand with a marble top which we used especially for pastry. I knew she found it a boring job, but this time it seemed to send her into a trance. She sprinkled the pastry with grated sharp cheddar cheese, folded it over, rolled it out again, sprinkled, rolled, sprinkled, rolled—far too many times.

"All right, that's enough," I had to say before she stopped. "You can cut it into strips now."

She blinked and seemed to shake herself. "Yes, of course." She gave a half-hearted smile. "Sorry, I got carried away."

You see? Gretel met my eye and gave a meaning nod. I just kept myself from nodding back. There was more than indigestion bothering Sidonie.

But it was not just Sidonie. Even Lexie had slipped into a solemn mood, attending to the blender mechanically while her mind appeared to be elsewhere.

"There!" Nick tossed a last potato into Gretel's bowl with an air of finality. "That's done!" He rose, stretched and began sauntering towards the door.

"*Now*—" Mona's voice stopped him—"you can bring in the crock of chicken livers, blot them on the kitchen towels,

wrap them in bacon and skewer them with cocktail sticks.''
Her tone brooked no argument. It was a messy, fiddly
task—and it was his.

Gretel beamed. It was the sort of chore that usually fell to
her. Lexie and Sidonie were still oblivious. I began to get a
bit worried.

"Lexie, that's blended enough. Turn it off."

"Sorry." She snapped it off and stood staring into space.
Sidonie went on slicing the pastry into oblong strips, using
an unnecessary amount of violence.

"Lightly, Sidonie. We don't want the marble carved, you
know." Mona shot me an anxious glance. Something was
wrong.

"Sorry." Sidonie flushed. It was seldom necessary to
correct or reprimand her; she wasn't used to it as the others
were. She bent again to her work, cutting lightly.

I wondered if she and Lexie had had a quarrel. Yet they
had seemed perfectly amicable as they arrived together.
Whatever the problem, they seemed more preoccupied than
seriously upset.

"Wakey, wakey!" Nick rushed in where Mona and I
were pussyfooting around. "You're both asleep on your
feet. What's the matter, Lexie—too much partying last
night?"

"I didn't sleep much," Lexie admitted. "Uncle Tristram
rang last night just before I went to bed. I've been wondering
how to tell you. It's all so awful." She shuddered, more
serious than I had ever seen her. Lexie usually took life very
lightly.

But not, perhaps, death. I knew instantly what she must
be talking about. Only one really awful thing had happened
lately.

"Mark Avery," I said.

"Yes. Uncle Tris said the police were there all day—long
after we left—going through Mark's office, examining everything, inspecting, measuring . . ." Her voice faltered. "And—
and—that's what makes it so awful. Even worse than it was.

"Oh, Jean, the police aren't sure it was an accident. They think someone might have tampered deliberately with the wall switch. They found the cover plate had been removed and the wires inside messed about so that too much current went through the electric razor when he switched it on—"

Gretel gave a horrified gasp. Nick turned pale green—he used an electric razor himself.

"And so," Lexie finished miserably, "Uncle Tris asked me to speak to you. He doesn't think the police will want to see any of us again, we were too far out of the way upstairs there—and besides, we only go there once a month to cook. But Uncle Tris wants us to try to remember if we ever noticed anything out of the ordinary at any time. If we did, we're to tell him."

Chapter
6

"No," I said, fighting sudden dizziness. "I didn't see anything. All I saw was Mark Avery." I had to cross abruptly to the rocking-chair and sit down while they clustered around me making soothing noises.

It was all right for Nick and Mona and Gretel; they hadn't been there. It wasn't even so bad for Lexie and Sidonie; although they had been with me at Quardon International, they hadn't seen the body.

But I had looked on Mark Avery lying dead in his office. I realized now how fortunate I'd been last night. Some self-protective mechanism had operated to blot out the memory and let me get a good night's sleep. I doubted that it would work tonight. Not now that I knew it hadn't been an accident; that, incredibly, one human being had done such a thing to another. And deliberately—that was the worst part. An angry blow might have been understandable, forgivable. But this had been cold-bloodedly planned in advance, prepared for; a deadly trap set and waiting, while somewhere a stealthy killer mixed with other men, laughing and joking—and waiting for his victim to walk into the trap.

Mark Avery was inextricably in my mind now and remained

there, haunting me for the rest of the day. For the first time, I wished that I did not have to work with food. Suddenly, I did not even want to look at it or think about it, far less concern myself with its preparation.

But, if I were feeling sick, how much sicker must they all be feeling at Quardon International?

By the time we arrived at the United Boroughs of New York Bank premises, my mood had improved. Mona had insisted on my taking a couple of aspirins and a rest that afternoon. I was ready to stop worrying about something I could not change and begin worrying about the reception.

"Now, remember, Gretel." I concentrated on the chief cause for concern. "Move slowly and smoothly. Don't overload your serving tray. Pay attention to what you're doing—"

"Yes, yes." She was radiant, an understudy being given her big chance because the star had broken a leg. All we could do was hope that Gretel wouldn't break anyone's leg.

"I will be very careful." She smoothed the frilly white apron tied over the black uniform. "I will watch you and do everything you do."

"Yes, well . . ." That idea made me slightly nervous, but I hesitated to give her *carte blanche* to use her own judgement. In the past, her judgement had not been particularly good. "Just do your best."

Lexie and Sidonie exchanged amused glances and fell in, one on either side of Gretel. "Come and take a quick look round with us," Lexie said. "We'll want to know where everything is, in case anyone asks us for directions."

"Everything?" Gretel was puzzled. She turned to watch Nick and Mona unpacking our containers. The food was here—what more could anyone possibly want?

"Cloakrooms, telephones, exits, parking lot—if any—all the usual offices." Lexie prodded her forward. "Come on, we haven't much time. The guests will be arriving."

"Go with them, Jean," Mona said softly, as they left the room. "I don't trust Lexie's sense of humour."

"Oh, but she wouldn't dream of doing anything to spoil this." I was certain of that. "It's a new account. She knows how important it is to us."

"She wouldn't think of it as having anything to do with us," Mona corrected me. "She'd think of it as a good joke on Gretel. Just keep an eye on her, I'll feel safer."

I moved off gratefully. Did Mona realize that the sight of food still made me feel faintly queasy? I'd be all right once the reception was in full swing and I had other things to think about. For the moment, I welcomed the excuse to get out of the small claustrophobic kitchen.

I caught up with them halfway down the corridor. Innocent as lambs. Not quite gambolling, but ready to at any moment. Lexie and Sidonie enjoyed the occasional receptions we catered for—the atmosphere was less formal than the luncheons and the eavesdropping usually a great deal more amusing—and Gretel was in the seventh heaven at being allowed to participate at last.

The Bank had a maisonette-type arrangement, subletting the ground and first floor of a business block in Knightsbridge. The ground floor housed the cashiers' desks and usual arrangements; the first floor was given over to the offices of the officers of the bank. Presumably, there was a vault or safe somewhere around the premises, but that was none of our business. We were only here to provide the buffet on the ground floor.

The buffet. That reminded me. I glanced nervously at Lexie. *Not* the floor show. But all appeared to be well. Which is to say, her uniform was buttoned demurely all the way up to the neck. I didn't bother to check the other two; I knew they'd be all right. It would not have occurred to them that we were in the heart of Millionaire-land and were about to mingle with some of the most influential people in international finance. If it had, they would have dismissed it with a shrug, unimpressed. It would be more important to them that the food was served at the right temperature and—in Gretel's case—did not slide off the serving tray to the floor just as the most important person in the room reached for a devilled drumstick.

We located and inspected the major points likely to be of interest, all of which appeared to be without surprises. Before returning to the kitchen, we tied a black bow around Gretel's right wrist so that she could remember which was left and which was right when she was giving directions.

Several bank officials stood clustered together waiting to greet the first arrivals. They nodded amiably to us as we passed.

Nick and Mona had set out shallow dishes of salted almonds, small bowls of dips and large bowls of crisps at strategic points around the room. Several desks had been pushed together and covered with tablecloths to form the bar. Again, salted almonds, dips and crisps were spaced at intervals along the length of this.

My eyes narrowed as I noticed a young man methodically walking along the impromptu bar and sampling our offering with a pseudo-connoisseur's air of being able to tell the country of origin of the salted almonds and the vintage of the dips. Only a wine merchant could carry off such a farce.

"I hope you like it," I slipped up behind him as he was trying not to choke on the dip Lexie had overdosed with tabasco. "It's only a nice little chilli grown on the North Slope of the Napa Valley during the dry season, but I think you'll be amused by its presumption."

"Really?" Eyes watering, he swallowed hard and tried to focus on me. "The caterer, I presume?"

"Mr. Stanley," I replied. I did not offer my hand.

"Uccello, actually," he said. "Aldo Uccello." Despite his name, his accent was impeccable. Second or third generation, presumably, and graduate of a very good university. Why did I find him so annoying?

"Couldn't the bank afford French wines?" I asked. "They didn't warn us they were doing this on the cheap."

"No need to be snobbish." His vision cleared and he beamed down on me. "We're all in the Common Market now."

"But some are more common than others." I turned and crossed over to Nick and Mona. Annoyingly, I could hear what sounded like a chuckle following me.

"Everything all right?" Mona greeted me.

"Yes, fine," I answered automatically, trying not to look back over my shoulder. "Why shouldn't it be?"

"Easy," Nick intervened. "Calm down. You don't have to snap Mona's head off. We're all on edge."

"I'm *not* on edge," I snapped.

"Look out!" Nick stiffened to attention, staring over my shoulder at something happening behind us. "Here come the first guests."

After that, it was modified chaos. Mona remained in the tiny kitchen, heating up the canapés to be served hot and filling the serving trays which we ran in and snatched up, swapping our empty trays for the full ones. It added to the awkwardness that the crew from the wine merchant's had set up shop on a table just outside the kitchen door and were juggling full and empty trays, as well. I narrowly averted collisions several times and the situation seemed to be so fraught with peril that I made Gretel remain in the reception area and took out her empty trays for refilling myself.

I was not particularly surprised to see that the wine merchant was not bothering to make any trips, or doing much of anything; he left all that to his minions. I only hoped it didn't give Nick ideas. One tradesman—however high class he considered himself—mingling with the guests instead of attending to duty was enough.

I was not consciously watching him, but I could not help noticing that he had stationed himself close by a large, vaguely familiar figure. They both had their backs to me and I caught my breath as Gretel approached them, balancing her tray carefully and offering it to them with a smile.

While the large man examined the tray closely, the young

man helped himself to a vol-au-vent. Almost immediately, the large man transferred his attention to his companion and watched him pop the vol-au-vent into his mouth, chew and swallow. After a judicious moment, he helped himself to three vol-au-vents and seemed to murmur something to his companion. The young man took a devilled drumstick and bit into it while the other was still working his way through the vol-au-vents.

Gretel looked puzzled, but kept smiling. Even when the large man began denuding the tray of all the drumsticks. She glanced around uncertainly, as though she would move away, but I caught her eye and shook my head, motioning her to stay where she was.

Ongar Manganian was not to be discouraged. If he wished to eat everything on Gretel's tray, the bank officials would not thank us for trying to stop him. There may have been guests present who were potentially more valuable clients for the bank, but there would not be many. This was no time to spoil the ship for a ha'porth of vol-au-vent. There was plenty of food and enough of us serving it. Let Ongar Manganian monopolize as many trays as he liked; the bank officials would just smile benevolently. This was why they were setting out the sprats to catch the mackerel, or, in this case, the whale.

Fortunately, I had recognized him in time. He had half-turned as someone had passed him and I was able to make the identification.

Gretel watched in fascination as he cleared her tray. I could see that she was struggling to keep from making some comment and I made my way hastily towards her. She had done awfully well so far and it would be a pity to blot her copybook now. Especially in front of Ongar Manganian.

Across the room, I spotted Lexie determinedly forging her way through the crowd in the same direction. Worse, she was not pausing when people indicated that they'd like something from her tray; in fact, she was pulling it away from them. Was it a coincidence, or had she sighted her quarry?

She had. As she came closer, I saw that her two top buttons were undone and she was wearing her most seductive smile. In the distance, I noticed Sidonie frowning.

Lexie was so intent upon projecting charm, personality— and availability—at Ongar Manganian as she approached that she didn't notice me until it was too late.

Gretel, on the other hand, was delighted to see me. Her tray was empty and she had been standing her ground in some confusion since I had plainly ordered her not to move.

"Gretel—" I took the empty tray from her hands and replaced it with my full one. "Take this—and circulate." I gave her a tiny push, sending her back into the crowd.

"Lexie—" I greeted her as she came up to us. "Take this—" I shoved Gretel's empty tray at her and removed her own tray from her hands—"and get it refilled. Hurry now—the people over in that corner haven't been attended to for quite some time. When you come back, start over there."

Looking daggers at me, she moved sullenly away. I knew that when she got to the kitchen Mona would take up the matter of the undone buttons. It wasn't going to be Lexie's evening—not if I could help it.

"Ah yes—the boss," Ongar Manganian said affably, to my surprise, recognizing me instantly. "You cover a great deal of territory in your endeavours."

"So do you," I said. Perhaps it was not so surprising. Although it seemed a much longer time, we had met only yesterday—and the events of that traumatic day were likely to be seared across all our memories for quite some time.

"And, once again, it is to you we are indebted for all this most excellent food." His eyes appraised my tray greedily.

It was enough to inspire greed in even a lesser man. There were plenty of marinated chicken livers wrapped in crispy bacon, hot and savoury; interspersed with these were hard-boiled eggs cut into thirds lengthwise, the yolks devilled with a pinch of curry and each one topped by the tiniest of parsley sprigs; for additional colour, as well as taste, there were pickled baby beets, cut in half and filled with softened cream cheese before being spread back together with the ubiquitous cocktail stick.

"How delicious it all looks," he murmured, making no effort to select anything, although his eyes sparkled. He turned to the young man beside him with a meaning look. "Does it not?"

"It does indeed." With elaborate casualness, the young man leaned across and took a chicken liver from the spot on the tray nearest to Ongar Manganian, the one I would have ordinarily expected Manganian to take. It struck me as slightly odd. Certainly it was peculiar, not to say rude, behaviour on the part of a wine merchant co-catering this reception.

"It is good, yes?" Ongar Manganian did not appear to take the behavior amiss. He watched intently as the young man savoured the delicacy, rolling it around in his mouth like rare wine. I was relieved when he finally swallowed it instead of spitting it out.

"Very good," the man pronounced. He smiled into my frown. "And I'm rather by way of being an expert on the subject. My family runs a restaurant in Soho."

"Really?" I said icily. It was surprising that he had not tried to arrange for them to do the food while he sewed up the liquor concession.

"I'm the black sheep of the family." He seemed to answer my unspoken thought. "One of them. Poor Mama and Papa—three fine sons and not one of us has followed them into the business. My eldest brother turned out to be an electronics wizard—I studied it for a bit, but it hadn't the fascination for me it had for him. My youngest brother went into education and is Deputy Headmaster of a Comprehensive now. That didn't interest me either, but I found I had my own talent. We've all gone our separate ways."

Ongar Manganian had been watching his face intently as

he spoke. Now he nodded and helped himself to a chicken liver . . . and another . . . and another. As he chewed approvingly, he gave the young man that meaning look again.

"I'm afraid—" Once more, he leaned across and selected one of the egg sections from a spot awkward for him but within easy reach for Ongar Manganian. "I'm afraid the young lady doesn't approve of me. She thinks I was critical of her dips. I was not—" He chewed, swallowed and continued. "They are excellent dips. The eggs are very good, too."

"Dips are sloppy food," Ongar Manganian said, a crumb of bacon clinging to his beard. "I do not like them." He frowned at the tray and picked up a curried egg. He nodded approvingly and began alternating the eggs with the chicken livers.

"I can assure you," the young man said, "you don't know what you're missing."

"I intend to miss nothing," Ongar Manganian said.

The young man grinned indulgently and took a beetball from beside Manganian's elbow. "Or perhaps she is old-fashioned," he said, "and thinks we should be properly introduced. Perhaps you might oblige. You seem to know her."

Ongar Manganian considered this proposition while his companion finished the beetball, then turned to me. "I am afraid I do not know your name."

"I'm Jean Ainley," I said. "Executive Meal Service."

"Excellent." Ongar Manganian took another beetball abstractedly. "Then I have much pleasure in introducing you to a rising young man in my employ. He is a financial genius and I am training him properly. Aldo Uccello—" He paused to chew and swallow.

"For now, Aldo is my right hand. My. . ." He groped for the more formal expression. "As Rodney Bletchley is to your Tristram Quardon. Aldo is my Personal Assistant."

"How do you do?" There was still something odd about this. Aldo Uccello was no Roddy Bletchley. But neither was he what I had originally concluded. "I'm sorry I seemed rude," I said. "I thought you were the wine merchant. I mean, I thought you should be on duty and not roaming around sampling the refreshments."

"A wine merchant he is not." Ongar Manganian spoke with authority. "But I can assure you he is very much on duty. I could not function without him." Having said which, he turned his full attention to my tray, depleting it rapidly and uninhibitedly.

Meanwhile, Aldo Uccello stood back and watched, making no move to take anything else. I realized abruptly that he had eaten one of everything offered, while his master watched intently. After Aldo had eaten with impunity, Ongar Manganian had then helped himself freely.

Personal Assistant, was he? Not so many centuries ago, in the land of Ongar Manganian's birth, there had been another and more realistic title for his post: *Official Taster*.

Chapter
7

"Special instructions." Released, but only on parole, I reported back to the kitchen. "More chicken livers, vol-au-vents and devilled drumsticks. Lots of them—he eats like a vacuum-cleaner."

"I don't know—" Mona wore the expression bordering on panic that usually set in at this stage of a reception. "I'm afraid we're running low—"

"Then several other people will have to go short. This is for Ongar Manganian. The bank won't thank us if we neglect *him*."

"Well . . ." Mona began to refill the tray reluctantly. There looked to be enough food still on hand. Inevitably, the less favoured items abounded. There were quantities of beetballs and stuffed eggs and pints of dip still left. Although we were getting low on the choicer items, I judged that we would have enough to see us through. The reception was at that full flood just before it starts to recede as people go on somewhere for dinner or depart for the theatre. But, just in case, it was time to give it a gentle push.

"Start sending out mostly cherry tarts from now on," I told Mona. "That ought to give them all a hint."

"Everything going well here?" One of the bank officials put his head round the door. "No problems?"

"Everything's fine." I told him what he wanted to hear which, in this case, was the truth. "I'm just getting a refill for Ongar Manganian. He asked for more of these especially." No harm in letting him know that one of his best prospects was enjoying the food enough to request more of special items.

"Oh, good, good!" He beamed approval. "That's the right idea. Keep him happy. He's a very important man."

"I know," I said, but he was gone. I smiled and shrugged at Mona, who finished filling up the tray with a more cheerful expression. I was just about to pick it up and depart when there was a rush of movement behind me.

"I think it's rotten of her! *Rotten!*" Sidonie slammed down her empty tray. "I'm sorry, Jean, Mona. I couldn't stop her, but I told her I wouldn't stand for it!"

"What's the matter?" I took a tighter grip on my tray, beset by visions of Lexie doing a striptease to attract Ongar Manganian's attention or, alternatively, of pouncing on him and—My vision gave out there. Not even my direct forebodings could imagine Lexie physically budging a bulk like that, far less dragging him off to her lair.

"Where's Nick?" Sidonie looked around wildly. "He's got to do something. Before it's too late!"

"He's just stepped out for a minute," Mona said, using the popular euphemism. "What's wrong? Has Gretel—?"

"No, no. It's Lexie. Lexie and her beasty Humpty. He's gate-crashed! Lexie's smuggled him in—I *told* her not to do it—and he's eating and drinking everything in sight. Someone from the bank is going to notice any minute. He stands out like a sore thumb—he's about twenty years younger than anyone else in the place. Nick's got to throw him out—fast!"

"Oh no! And just as everything was going so well!" I set down my tray, then remembered that Ongar Manganian was waiting for it.

"Here—" I caught it up again and thrust it at Sidonie. "Take this and go and dance attendance on Ongar Manganian. Let him eat it all—even the tray cloth, if he feels so inclined. But *don't* let Lexie near him!"

"I understand," Sidonie said unexpectedly. She gave me the sort of look to make me feel that she did understand. I wondered how much she had to put up with from Lexie along those lines. It couldn't be easy to be the plain flatmate, dragged along as part-chaperone, part-companion for the sake of whatever passed for propriety in their circles and standing by ignored while Lexie turned full voltage on any eligible males in the vicinity.

Sidonie took the tray and whisked away, leaving me staring blankly after her for a moment.

"Lexie—" Mona broke the spell. "If we ran a genuine school, we'd have to consider expelling her."

"But we don't," I reminded her. "And we can't." We would not only lose the money pouring into our coffers for Lexie's tuition—and possibly Sidonie's—but we would risk antagonizing our oldest and best client, her Uncle Tristram.

"I know," she sighed. "You'd better go out and see what you can do. I'll send Nick out to help you as soon as he comes back."

I nodded and returned to the reception. I had no trouble spotting Lexie's Humpty, although I had never met him. As Sidonie had noted, he was at least twenty years younger than most of the other guests. He was also the second largest male in the room; second only to Ongar Manganian himself. Looking at the large ovoid shape, one immediately saw why his given name of Humphrey had been transposed so aptly into Humpty.

And he was heading for a fall.

Automatically, I scanned the room as I moved across it. Gretel, frowning with concentration, had not dropped anything, spilled anything, or collided with anyone—yet. A quiet pride was beginning to radiate from her as her confidence grew. If she got through the rest of the evening without mishap, we would have to consider letting her help at Directors' Luncheons. It might not be a bad idea. A spell in the kitchen after this escapade might even get it through to Lexie that she had gone too far. Letting Gretel replace her would underline her disgrace.

Sidonie, as instructed, was standing before Ongar Manganian while he systematically depleted her tray. I noticed that a couple of bank officials had joined him, but they were wise enough not to get between him and the refreshments, nor to take any themselves. Although she maintained a professional smile, Sidonie's worried gaze followed me as I advanced on Humpty.

Lexie was watching from a far corner, half-hidden behind a cluster of guests. When she saw my head turn in her direction, she moved to one side so that she was completely concealed. I knew that she was still watching, though.

Humpty was unaware of my approach. He had marked out a corner of a desk for himself with a bowl of dip, crisps, celery and napkin containing four drumsticks. By his elbow, there were three empty glasses. He was holding out the empty glass in his hand to one of the wine waiters for a refill as I reached him. I stood there silently for a moment, looking at him.

The Hon. Humphrey had some double-barrelled name I had never quite caught. Lexie invariably referred to him as Humpty. He was one of her regular escorts. Too impecunious to be of any real interest to her, he was the one she fell back on when there was nothing more promising in the offing. Although financially ineligible, he amused her. There was another fairly regular escort, too—what was his name? I glanced around, but Humpty seemed to be the only intruder and Sidonie hadn't mentioned anyone else.

One was enough. Too many. Clients weren't going to patronize a catering service which ran in its own freeloaders at their expense. It was time to get rid of Humpty—and quickly. I looked back, but there was no sign of Nick. It looked as though I was going to have to throw him out by myself. There was no more time to waste, he was already beginning to attract some curious glances.

He turned his head suddenly and we were eyeball to eyeball. Furthermore, he knew it. I could see it in the way his face changed. The slack-lipped grin gave way to something more truculent.

"All right," I told him. "Out! The party's over!"

"I beg your pardon?" He tried to bluff it through.

"Out!" I repeated.

"Me? Are you talking to me?" His voice began to rise. He looked around for support, but Lexie wasn't going to show herself until the crisis was over. "Do you know who I am?"

"Yes," I said. "And that's why you're leaving."

"Now see here—" he began to bluster. "I'll have you know—"

"Spot of bother?" a quiet voice asked at my elbow. I turned gratefully, but it was not Nick. Ongar Manganian's personal assistant had come up behind me and it looked as though he were going to lend me some of his assistance.

"Gate-crasher," I said briefly. "I've asked him to leave."

"Very wise of you." Aldo Uccello ran an expert eye over Humpty. "I wouldn't say he was adding anything to the tone of the occasion."

"I don't know who you think you are—" Humpty glared at him wildly. "But—"

"Aldo Uccello." Aldo extended his hand and Humpty automatically took it before realizing what a bad idea that was. He was drawn forward inexorably.

"Suppose we step outside and I will explain further." Aldo dropped his arm casually around Humpty's shoulders, the grip of his hand changed slightly and Humpty gasped with pain. It was smoothly—expertly—done. No one else at the reception was aware that anything was happening except that two of the youngest guests were strolling out of the room in a friendly manner.

Except for Ongar Manganian, that is. I saw the slight turn

of his head and knew that he had missed nothing and was unsurprised by the turn of events. Possibly it was he who had sent Aldo Uccello to my aid. Just in case, I sent him a fleeting smile of gratitude, which was half-acknowledged by a nod before he returned to his conversation with the bankers.

His personal assistant was a man of curious talents. There had been an unnerving expertise in the way he had removed Humpty. It was obviously not the first time he had performed such little services. I trusted they stopped short of taking Humpty for a ride—his transgression had not been that serious. But it shed an interesting new light on Aldo Uccello: as well as Official Taster, it seemed that he was also a bodyguard.

I hoped that he didn't include acting as a hit man among his many little chores.

Chapter

8

It was generally agreed that the reception had been a success, but the next day was Saturday and there was no time to rest on our laurels. It was the busiest day for Portobello Road Market and we had many good customers among the stallholders who would be looking for us. Apart from which, there was always a goodly sum to be scooped up from the casual trade. It was a major tourist area and, while the faces were constantly changing, they also got hungry and had full pockets. A few hours on duty there did wonders for our cash flow problems.

Nick occasionally grumbled that we ought to give up the Portobello route now that we were moving up into the more rarified strata of City Boardrooms. But we hadn't risen high enough yet to be above the need to pay our suppliers and it could take a long time for our invoices to be processed through financial departments before clients eventually sent out payment to us. A Saturday working Portobello provided the financing for most of the luncheons we would serve the following week.

Today, however, Nick was not only helping to unload the van, he had offered to come along with me. It wasn't quite unheard of, but he usually avoided this duty for fear of being seen by one of his advertising friends. Being Director of Executive Meal Service carried snob appeal; being caught filling pitta bread pockets for the queue at the tailgate of a van was too down-market to be contemplated.

"Are you sure this will be enough?" Dubiously, he surveyed the crocks of pâté, the large bowls of egg mayonnaise, chicken salad, tuna salad, the piles of presliced meats and loaves of buttered brown and white bread and stacks of halved pitta bread.

"If it isn't, we can always come back for more." I wrestled the tub—light, but awkward—of green salad (shredded lettuce, endive and fennel) into its place at the rear of the van.

Mona came out carrying a large plastic container of grated cheese. "Don't forget this." She handed it to me and stepped back, looking at Nick accusingly.

"I'll just go and get the coffee urn," he said. "Then we should be ready, shouldn't we?"

"I thought," Mona said coldly, "that you and I were going in to town to look at wallpaper samples and choose the paint today."

"You don't want to go into the West End today," Nick protested. "It will be too crowded. Everyone will be trying to get at the sample books, the salespeople will be rushed off their feet and won't have time to attend to us properly. No, we'll go on Monday when it's quiet and we can take our time choosing what we want."

"Well . . ." Mona was clearly wavering.

"Besides—" He spoiled it by adding: "Today I've got to see a man about some chairs."

"I might have known it!" Mona exploded. "All your promises never—"

"The coffee urn—" Nick disappeared at high speed, voice trailing over his shoulder. "I'll be right back."

"Your brother!" Mona turned to me for support. "I don't know how you ever put up with him for a lifetime!" Her face changed in a way that made me suddenly nervous. "I don't know how much longer I'm going to be able to."

"He's very keen on the idea," I defended. "I don't really see that it matters whether you get the wallpaper or the chairs first. He'll carry through and finish the whole project as soon as he can."

"It's not that," Mona sighed. "It's just that he's always promising more than he can deliver. Half the time, he has no intention of doing whatever it is, but he promises anyway. Just to keep people quiet. I wish he wouldn't, but I can't break him of the habit."

"He was always like that." I remembered the occasions as a child when I had waited for my elder brother to come home from school and take me to the cinema or down to the shops for an ice-cream, or whatever it was he had promised to do. Waited and waited, while the shadows lengthened and the sick feeling in my stomach grew as I gradually realized that he had forgotten all about me and gone off on some more interesting concern of his own. Inevitably, I had learned that "promise" was only a word to Nick, not a concept as it was to other people. It made for a bumpy childhood, but had been good basic training for adult life. Mona, however, had been the only child of an adoring father. She was learning her lesson about male promises comparatively late in life.

"I suppose it's just the way Nick is made." I sighed, too.

"Here we are." Nick returned, wheeling along the large coffee urn on its metal trolley. "I'm afraid I'll need a hand getting this into the van," he said to Mona.

She turned on her heel and stalked back to the house. The door slammed behind her.

"What's the matter with her?" Nick looked after her with a surprised expression.

"You *did* promise." That was all I was going to say; it brought back too many reminders of my childhood.

"I meant at the first opportunity," Nick said. "This isn't

an opportunity, it's a working day. Mona ought to be more reasonable.''

Nick joined me on my Saturday round so infrequently that it was quite reasonable of Mona to expect him to go with her instead, but I forbore from pointing this out.

"You know—" He frowned abstractedly at the wheels of pizza and quiche lorraine in the makeshift rack hung from the back of the passenger seat. "We ought to have a different type of van if you want to operate a mobile canteen. Something more professional—with cooking facilities. We could do hot sausages, toasted sandwiches—''

"Let's leave that to the pubs," I said. "The customers are quite happy with things the way they are." I slammed and latched the rear door and went round to the front. Nick was already in the driver's seat. "Besides, I thought you wanted to give up this side of the business and concentrate on the executive meals."

"Yes, but we ought to be sensible." He drove into the road and headed towards the market. "I mean, this brings in quite a decent whack each week, doesn't it?"

"It helps to keep us solvent," I admitted.

"There you are!" He lifted one hand from the wheel in an expansive gesture. "And that's just one van. Think what we could do with two."

"What I'm thinking," I said truthfully, "is that Mona would kill you. You promised her that the next car you bought would be a saloon. You know she hates the shooting brake."

"But we need it," Nick said plaintively, quite as though I had ever argued that fact. "You know we do. Mona would hate even more—" he gave a short laugh—"climbing over sacks of potatoes and onions piled into a saloon."

"I know," I said. "But you can't blame her for being upset at times. This business has rather taken over her life. She wants something of her own. Something that isn't tax deductible or off the expense account."

"Mona never complained about the expense account

when I was at the Agency." Nick sounded a trifle bitter. "She still wants all the luxuries, but she's got to learn that she can't dictate her own terms any more."

"I'm just warning you," I said.

"She won't leave me," Nick said confidently. "Besides, what I have in mind might be something she'd approve of. We could use it for holidays and save on hotel bills. If we had one, we could make a few ferry trips over to France and combine a short break with loading up with cheeses and delicacies and our duty-free allowances. She'd like that, all right."

"Just the same . . ."

"Ah, she'll come round." He had no doubts. "And it wouldn't be all that expensive. A second-hand motor caravan. If you know what you're doing—and I'll take old Pete with me, he's an expert mechanic—you can pick one up at a good price. Sunday morning, down Kingsway around Australia House. All those Aussies who've been over here doing Europe and want to go back home are lined up with their motor caravans trying to sell them off to the newest contingent of Aussies who've just arrived. They don't mind if the occasional Pommie steps in—as long as he's got the ready. We ought to be able to pick up something decent at a knockdown price. Then we can just convert it a bit, make more room to carry food and cook it, perhaps another cooking unit and a second tank of Calor gas—"

"That would mean you had to take out the bunks." I brought him down to earth. "Then you wouldn't be able to sleep in it when you went to the Continent."

"We could re-convert it," he said testily. "It would be quite simple, really. Don't make mountains out of molehills."

"Think of it as a dress rehearsal for explaining the project to Mona," I told him. "*She'll* think of all these objections, never fear."

"Ah, Mona." He sighed heavily. It began to sound as though the bloom was off the rose for both of them.

"Mona . . . well, Mona will just have to adjust to a few things. *You* think it's a good idea, don't you?"

I could not deny it. I was in favour of anything that would help Executive Meal Service to grow and expand. I was especially in favour of something that would mean consolidating and enlarging our already lucrative cash trade. With two vehicles, we could cover a second string of street markets, those usually serviced only by the ubiquitous hot dog and hamburger vans. Our experience had already proved that stallholders and public alike were delighted to be offered a better variety of more expensive and flavourful foods.

"Don't you?" I had not replied quickly enough.

"I think it's a super idea," I said. "I just can't help thinking about what Mona will say."

"Leave Mona to me," he said shortly.

On Sunday morning, Edda Price rang up. She had my private telephone number, which was not the one printed on the Executive Meal Service business card, but the separate telephone in my upstairs flat.

"I'm sorry to disturb you," she said, sounding crisp, efficient and not at all sorry. "I wouldn't have done so if it weren't urgent."

"Of course." I tried to sound sympathetic and alert. It took a moment before I could focus on my watch. It couldn't be eight-thirty! Perhaps I'd forgotten to wind it. I held it to my ear, where it ticked relentlessly.

"I was sure you wouldn't mind." Equally relentlessly, Edda Price thrummed into my other ear. "I thought it best to get this settled as soon as possible."

"Yes." I stifled a yawn. "What is it?"

"It's terribly short notice, I know, but it can't be helped." That was obviously as much of an apology as I was going to get. "Tomorrow. We're having a Special Board Meeting to . . ." For the first time, her voice faltered. "To settle the question of who's going to take Mark Avery's place on the board.''

"Already?" The word slipped out before I could stop it, I was so startled.

"I agree," she said. "I think it's in the worst possible taste. I want to assure you that Quardon International had nothing to do with it. It has been *forced* on us by our new... associate. Mr. Manganian has to go out of the country on business and he wishes to leave his own nominee on the Board. Some Italian man, although I believe he was born in this country—"

"Aldo Uccello," I said. "His personal assistant."

"Personal hatchet man!" For a moment, the old Edda spoke. "You know him?"

"I've met him," I said. "They were both at the reception at the United Boroughs of New York Bank the other night."

"*Were* they?" I could almost hear the click as the information registered and was filed away for future reference. "Then you can see it wouldn't do at all. Tristram Quardon is going to fight it—he wants Roddy on the Board instead. *Much* more suitable. Oh, but it's all so appalling—" Her voice cracked and once again I glimpsed the broken woman sprawled on the carpet in Mark Avery's office. "*Squabbling* like this when... when Mark isn't even in his grave yet!"

"I imagine the funeral will be private," I said.

"Yes. Yes, just the family—his wife and two sons—and a few close friends... Tristram... myself..." I heard her catch a deep painful breath and blow her nose.

"And tomorrow—" It wasn't quite changing the subject, but it brought her back to a less emotive level. "How many for lunch?"

"Yes, the Board," she said gratefully. "I'm not sure how many will be there. Not all of them. The meeting was called so suddenly. Some of them had other engagements—"

And some of them didn't want to get caught in the middle of a power struggle between Tristram Quardon and Ongar

Manganian. They couldn't be blamed for that—it was a no-win situation.

"*About* how many do you expect?" I prompted, beginning to do a little mental arithmetic on my own. Certainly Tristram Quardon and Ongar Manganian would be there, also Roddy Bletchley and probably Aldo Uccello. That made four, and Edda to take the Minutes made five . . ."

"There may be twelve," she said uncertainly. "Or thirteen." She gave a sort of cough that was meant to pass as a laugh. "With the things that have happened lately, that would be apposite, wouldn't it?"

"What would you like for lunch?" I ignored the rhetorical question and asked a more practical one of my own.

"I don't know," she said. "I don't care. I doubt if anyone else will. Food isn't very important at a time like this. Except—" there was an abrupt jarring viciousness in her tone—"to Ongar Manganian!"

"Something simple," I said, calculating rapidly. Simple enough to be reassuring to the others and not make them feel guilty because they were living high when Mark Avery had been struck low . . . but something that would be impressive to Ongar Manganian.

"Steak-and-kidney pie?" I suggested. Oysters could be added, as in the Old English recipes, without detracting from the security food aspect for the English Directors, but the touch of luxury would serve to signal to Ongar Manganian that he was getting a dish slightly above the ordinary. Mashed potatoes could be stretched out if more than expected arrived and were thus safer than new potatoes. Spring greens were at their best now and would also be reassuring as well as delicious.

"Oh, I suppose so," she sighed. "They won't want anything elaborate. It wouldn't seem right."

"No sweet, but a good cheese board," I said. The lack of a sweet would provide a touch of austerity, tempered by a lavish cheese board, which most of them would prefer in the circumstances.

"Yes, yes." Her heart wasn't in it. "I'll leave it to you. So long as you can do it, that's all that I was worried about."

"We'll fit you in," I said diplomatically. No point in letting her know that we had nothing else scheduled tomorrow. "Of course, as it's such short notice, we may not be able to bring our usual waitresses—" This would be the ideal opportunity to slip Gretel into the active team and leave Lexie back in the kitchen doing the donkey work. The fact that it was Quardon International would emphasize to her that her wrist was being well and truly slapped for Friday's escapade.

"That doesn't matter," Edda said. "Who's going to notice?"

She had a point. Despite Lexie's fond hopes, the servitors were, for the most part, the original invisible people. There was the classic story, which surfaced at intervals with only the name of the world-famous actor changing, of the actor who disappeared from the table during a formal dinner, borrowed the waiter's jacket and served the next two courses to his friends without being noticed. No one ever paid any attention to the form hovering over one's chair dispensing the food.

"We'll be there early," I said. "Just in case there are any problems."

There was a short silence and I wondered if I had been tactless. After the last luncheon at Quardon, there was little that could be considered a problem.

"That's fine . . ." Her attention seemed to have wandered elsewhere. I remembered that there was supposed to be an invalid husband in the background; one of the reasons she had done so well at Quardon. A person who is not too anxious to go home doesn't mind long hours of overtime.

"Just do as you think best." She rang off.

Chapter
9

Everyone was in the kitchen when I returned from the fishmonger's with the oysters in the morning. The fragrance of toasting sesame seeds hung in the air and Gretel was in her accustomed corner grating cheese. We used the days when there were no luncheons scheduled to catch up on all the little tasks that would expedite our work when we were busy. I knew Mona had planned to cook for the freezer today and so I had left a note telling her of our change of plans.

She had found the note. Two large pans stood waiting to be filled while she cut up and mixed the steak and kidney.

"Here you are." I dropped the parcel of oysters on her table and went to wash and change.

When I returned, Nick was struggling with the oysters. He was getting to be quite expert; furthermore, I had a sneaking suspicion that he enjoyed it all far more than he admitted. It was one thing to be theoretically knowledgable about a field and quite another to roll up your sleeves and earn your expertise. I also suspected that he played up this angle for all it was worth when he met his old advertising colleagues for the occasional pub crawl. Not that anyone—

except Mona—could blame him for that. It had been traumatic for him to have been suddenly declared redundant, although it was happening all around him. Not all his friends had fallen on their feet in the catlike way Nick had. But not all his friends had obliging younger sisters already self-employed in a promising business that needed only a fresh infusion of capital and labour to expand and flourish.

By this time, Nick's friends had probably forgotten that he had waited to collect his golden handshake—and he wouldn't be reminding them. It made a better story that way. Everyone knows the secret of success in business lies in the ability to move up to a better job one step ahead of being given the push at your old company. If any of them remembered, Nick had probably convinced them that he had actually started me off in business and had been biding his time in order to collect his golden handshake before joining me.

It was too bad that Mona couldn't enter into the spirit of the project as wholeheartedly as we had. She was dealing with the oysters now as though they were personal enemies who had done her an unforgivable injury. I restrained a wince as she hurled them into the pie mixture and looked away. It would be both pointed and insulting to offer to take over from her at this stage. I would just have to place my trust in the fact that her end results were almost always perfect, despite the way she occasionally treated the ingredients.

"Gretel—" I turned thankfully to someone whose only problem was trying to grate the cheddar without also grating her fingernails into the bowl. Gretel might be clumsy, but at least she was uncomplicated.

"Gretel, would you like to come with us to Quardon today? You can start learning the Boardroom luncheon routine."

"Me?" Gretel's face lit up. "*Me?*" (Would Cinderella like to go to the Ball?) "Today? So soon?"

"You did very well at the reception Friday evening." I hoped that didn't sound too patronizing, but Gretel seemed to be taking it in the spirit in which it was meant. "It's time you began getting a bit more practice."

"I would love this!" Gretel attacked the grater vigorously with the remaining nub of cheese. "Oh!" She gave a sudden scream of dismay. "My fingernail!"

"It's all right." Restraining a wince, I spooned up the nail fragment and surrounding shreds of cheese. "You can borrow my nail file. Leave the rest of the cheese, someone else can finish up, and go and change into your uniform."

It was really too early, Mona was just putting the pies into the oven, but Gretel needed to calm down before she would be of any more use in the kitchen. I glanced at my watch as Gretel left the room. Where were the other girls? It was past their usual arrival time. Had they run into a traffic jam along the way?

Outside, the day was grey and chill. Last week's brief promise of spring had disappeared as though it had never existed.

The mood of the Quardon Directors would be about as bleak as the weather. Oxtail soup, I decided, taking the containers from the deep freeze. No frills, all security food today. It might provide some obscure comfort after what sounded as though it were going to be a very sticky Board meeting. No one was going to be anxious to welcome Ongar Manganian's representative on to the Board. At the same time, not everyone would welcome Roddy Bletchley, either. Oh, why did Mark Avery have to die just when things were going so well?

Mark Avery had had to die because he was in someone's way. The grim answer came unbidden and I shuddered convulsively.

"Careful," Nick warned. "You could catch pneumonia bending over an icy deep-freeze all day."

"It's not that icy." His words pinpointed the vague unease I had been feeling before the thought of Mark Avery had crowded it out. It returned in full force now. I pinched the polythene bag anxiously, but the soup seemed solid enough. Nevertheless . . .

Food poisoning is the nightmare threat that must always lurk at the back of the minds of anyone dealing with food, whether they be professional caterers or hostesses in private homes. Odourless, colourless, tasteless, silent . . . sometimes deadly. Undetectable—until the first victim collapses.

"It's all right, isn't it?" Anxiety, fuelled by guilt, propelled Nick and Mona to my side instantly. We needed a new freezer; that should take priority over a second van or even doing up the dining-room. We had bought this one second-hand, as a stopgap measure, and had been nursing it along ever since. It was a dangerous thing to do, but we had got away with it . . . so far.

"I think so." Mona moved her hand around inside the cabinet, testing the temperature. "But, just to be on the safe side . . ." She lowered the thermostat another notch.

We could not go on like this much longer. The risk was too great. Harmful bacteria could form and grow too easily. Constant vigilance was necessary. In Great Britain alone, about five thousand cases of enteritis are notified each year caused by *Salmonellae*. Even though few of those cases are fatal, that's an awful lot of discomfort—which can last from one to eight days—and a lot of lost reputations among the people inadvertently responsible.

Rarer in occurrence, but producing one of the most poisonous toxins known, is *Clostridium botulinum*; the neurotoxin acts on the central nervous system and the effect is usually fatal. The victims can take from twenty-four hours up to eight days to die. The lucky ones can take over eight months to recover. That one didn't bear thinking about. Nevertheless, there were occasional outbreaks.

"I'm sure it's all right," Nick said positively. Mona and I exchanged glances. He knew less than either of us about the dangers, nor had he ever taken any trouble to learn them, as we had. He was still immersed in his advertising world when we had taken the necessary courses and had never bothered to remedy his deficiencies along those lines.

"Is anything wrong?"

We looked up to find that Lexie and Sidonie had entered silently while we had been bending over the freezer cabinet. A vaguely familiar figure lurked behind them as though trying to hide.

"Nothing." We moved away hastily. At some point, it would be proper to give the girls a lecture on bacteria and the dangers of food poisoning, but discretion demanded that we wait until we were beyond stone-throwing range ourselves. After we had bought our new, first-class freezer, we could be sanctimonious about the problem.

"Never mind." Sidonie shrugged out of her coat, unexpectedly taking charge. "Humphrey has something to say to you. And so has Lexie." She turned to face the culprits. "Come along, now."

"Like to apologize . . ." Humphrey shuffled forward, mumbling. "No harm intended . . . Just a joke . . ." He ran out of steam and threw Lexie a look of desperate appeal. He was not accustomed to apologizing for his actions.

"Really," Lexie pouted. "I don't know why Sidders—"

"Sidonie!" Sidonie corrected sternly.

"I don't know why *Sidonie*—" Lexie sighed deeply and started over—"is making all this fuss. Humpty was *my* guest the other night and—"

"When you're paying the bill, you can invite the guests." It might sound harsh, but it was time to make the position clear. Lexie had too many impecunious friends to be allowed to get away with ideas like that.

"All right, I'm *sorry*," Lexie said grudgingly, one eye on Sidonie. "How was I to know everyone would be so *stuffy* about it?"

Common sense should have told her; but that was not a commodity Lexie had ever felt the need of. She had other ways of getting what she wanted. She left common sense to plain practical people like Sidonie.

"We've picked up an unexpected assignment for today—"
I spoke across Lexie to Sidonie. "Quardon International are
having an unscheduled Board meeting. I thought we'd take
Gretel along and give her some practical experience. She
did very well the other night. Lexie—" I answered the
unspoken question—"can stay here and help Mona this
afternoon."

"Oh no!" Lexie cried. "It's not fair! Uncle Tris will be
expecting to see me. Besides, Gretel will just make a mess
of everything, you *know* she will. It was only a fluke that
she didn't do anything wrong the other night."

There was a suppressed snort of laughter from Humpty.
He had been wandering about the kitchen as we talked, his
greedy, gleaning eyes alert for anything he could nibble. I
had watched as he had dipped his fingers into the bowl of
shredded cheese, but was too busy dealing with Lexie at
that moment to take on Humpty as well.

"I don't know why you think it's so funny!" Lexie
whirled on Humpty and then saw that he was not reacting
to her plight; in fact, he had been unaware of it. His
attention was elsewhere.

Pinned up over Mona's workplace were some old American cartoons, yellowing with age, which Nick had brought
back from one of his trips to New York. One depicted a
hostess at a dinner-party passing round a dish to her bemused guests. The caption read: "*I'll never forget the last
time I served mushrooms—ambulances all over the place!*"

I gave a last worried look at the freezer and moved away.
This was one of the days when the cartoon failed to amuse
me.

Another drawing showed a salesman handing over a new
pressure cooker to a male customer and saying: "*A word of
warning, lest you forget the instructions and blow your fool
head off.*" There was also one of a man who had got his
necktie hopelessly entangled in an eggbeater, with his wife
commenting: "*Oh, fine. I must call on you for help more
often.*"

Humpty stopped snickering, puzzled by Lexie's abrupt attack. He had been reading the cartoons, not listening to our conversation and the nuances of Lexie's situation had escaped him.

"It was all *your* fault, anyway!" Lexie had realized her mistake and her fury increased, still directed at a bewildered Humpty.

"It was *his* idea—" She appealed to me. "He thought it would be fun to sneak in and get a free feed. Oh, *please*, can't I come with you today?"

I might have weakened but just then Gretel returned, neat and tidy in her uniform—with every button firmly done up. No nonsense there. "I am all ready," she said proudly.

"So you are." I met Lexie's eye and she saw that her cause was lost.

"Oh, all right," she said sulkily, dividing a glare between Gretel and Humpty. "But Humpty can stay here with me and do his share of the work. Nick—" she added nastily— "will be glad to have someone else to peel the potatoes."

Humpty didn't seem to mind. He had resumed his wandering and was bearing down on the larder like a homing pigeon.

"We can always use an extra pair of hands." I moved to cut him off before he reached the larder door. "Why don't I find you a spare apron and you can sit over here."

"Yes. All right. Yes." Humpty allowed himself to be led to Gretel's empty corner. He inhaled deeply as the aroma of steak-and-kidney pie began floating through the room. One could almost see his salivary glands working.

"Never mind the potatoes," Mona said briskly. "He can peel apples. I thought we'd do a few deep-dish apple pies for the freezer this afternoon."

A glazed smile spread over Humpty's face. I began to suspect it might be easier to co-opt him than get rid of him.

Perhaps Lexie suspected it, too. Her baleful expression deepened. She had intended Humpty to share her disgrace and sense of punishment; instead he was beaming with delight. He had obviously deduced, correctly, that he was in line for a working lunch and would have the added perk of dipping into any food that came his way.

Mona and I exchanged glances and she nodded. She'd keep an eye on Humpty and make sure that he sang sufficiently for his supper. Nick was transparently amused by the situation and turned away before Lexie noticed it and transferred some of her fury to him.

Sidonie had disappeared to change into her own uniform. It was still a bit early, but Gretel was in hers and I suspected that Sidonie was not above wishing to underline Lexie's disfavour.

I removed a selection of cheeses from the fridge so that they could begin warming up to room temperature in good time for serving, and started collecting the things we would need for the luncheon. Gretel carried the serving board and cheese wire out to the van; even though she seemed to be improving, there was no point in tempting fate by letting her carry anything breakable or spillable.

Mona opened the oven door to check the progress of the pies. Nick would load those into the van in about another half-hour; the crust was already turning a delicate golden brown. I glanced at my watch, everything was moving along in perfect timing.

"That smells good," Sidonie came back into the kitchen, looking crisp and efficient but with an air of suppressed excitement.

"Good enough to eat," Nick said cheerfully. "Pity it's destined for the Boardroom bellies, I could do with a bit of it myself."

Humpty's face fell. Up to then, he had obviously thought it was on his luncheon menu.

"Perhaps there'll be some left," I said. "We're not sure how many will turn up, so we may have overcooked."

"I thought we'd have sukiyaki ourselves." Mona slammed the oven door shut. She got a chunk of rump steak from the fridge and carried it back to her table. Humpty watched the swift, sure movements of her gleaming knife in fascination as she expertly slivered the steak into thin strips. He was making heavy weather with the paring knife allotted to him and someone else was going to have to core the apples if we wanted anything left of them at all.

"Never mind that for a moment," Sidonie said. "Mona, Jean, Nick—" She darted a sudden suspicious glance at her cousin. "Lexie hasn't told you our news, has she?"

Lexie wasn't telling us anything. She had withdrawn into a fit of smouldering sulks and hunched in her corner moodily stabbing at a large potato.

"It's *so* super." Reassured, Sidonie continued. "I didn't want to tell you before because I didn't want you to get your hopes up, but it's all right now. We've brought it off! We've got you the catering contract for the Charity Ball next month!"

"Marvellous!" I cheered before Mona could speak. I could see her opening her mouth to ask, "*What charity ball?*," but that was irrelevant. I knew that Sidonie worked for several charities in her spare time and one thing might lead to another. I discounted entirely her polite "*we*." Lexie might have been dragooned into an occasional appearance at a committee meeting or a minimal subscription, but Sidonie would have been the moving spirit for anything actually achieved.

"I had to give them an estimated quotation, since we wanted to surprise you. But you can confirm it now—" Sidonie pulled a folded piece of paper from her pocket. "I don't think I was too far out."

"It looks bang on." I studied the scribbled figures. Sidonie had been learning far more than I had thought.

"What precisely—" Mona came round to read over my shoulder—"does this entail?"

"Oh, you know the sort of thing," Sidonie said airily, forgetting that everyone wasn't familiar with her world. For a moment, she bore an uncanny resemblance to Lexie. "Everyone will be going to private supper-parties beforehand. The Ball will start about 9 p.m. There'll be lashings of champagne and they'll expect sandwiches and strawberries and cream around midnight. Then they'll draw the prizes, more champagne and dancing, and perhaps half of them will go home. The main thing is the buffet breakfast at about 4 a.m. or so."

"Buffet breakfast . . ." Mona murmured thoughtfully. "Country-house style, I suppose . . ."

"That's it," Sidonie said. "Lots of chafing dishes set out along a trestle table. Probably about a hundred and fifty or so will stay on for breakfast."

"A hundred and fifty," Mona echoed weakly, but rallied almost immediately. "Scrambled eggs, I suppose. Masses of scrambled eggs . . ."

"Sausages, grilled mushrooms, devilled kidneys," I took up the refrain, thinking aloud. "And kedgeree . . . lots of kedgeree. Yes, we should be able to manage."

"Don't forget—" Lexie interrupted nastily. "You'll have to hire some extra people to help with the serving. This time, Sidonie and I will be *guests*."

I was shocked at the sight of Tristram Quardon. He was pale and gaunt, as though layers of flesh had melted away collapsing his skin back on to the skeleton frame, emphasizing the skull structure just beneath the surface.

Alas, poor Yorick . . . alas, poor Mark . . . alas, poor Tristram. Everyone was a loser at a time like this.

He popped his head round the door and gave a wan smile at the preparations going on. He nodded briefly to me, looked at Sidonie and Gretel, and disappeared again. If he had noticed Lexie's absence, he had evidently decided not to remark on it. He had enough problems today.

Hard on his heels—as was only to be expected—came Edda Price. She was looking better, but she could have hardly looked worse than the last time I had seen her. As though aware of this, she was almost aggressively efficient.

"We're going in now. We shouldn't be long. The only item on the agenda is . . . is Mark's replacement. There'll be seventeen for lunch. Not all of them," she added disapprovingly, "members of the Board." Of course, they would have to feed the unsuccessful candidate—that ought to make for an interesting lunch.

"Lunch will be ready when you are," I said as soothingly as I dared. "It won't matter if it takes longer than you think, or if they linger over drinks afterwards."

We put the pies into the oven at a comfortable temperature and the pot of soup on top of the stove to simmer. The spring greens could be put on to cook as we served the soup.

Everything was under control in the kitchen; I wondered if the same could be said for anywhere else in the building. There was a feeling of sickness, of muted hysteria, in the air. Secretaries and typists still gathered in gossiping knots in the hallways, looking over their shoulders and jumping at sudden loud noises. As I passed the typing pool on my way in, an ambulance had gone by outside, klaxon wailing. There had been abrupt silence in the typing pool; it was easy to visualize the hands suspended above the keyboards... waiting. Gradually, as the sound of the ambulance died away in the distance and the typists realized that Quardon International had not been its destination, the typing started again and the crescendo of sound returned to normal. Until the next ambulance or police car was heard approaching...

I had Sidonie set the plates and glasses round the table while Gretel arranged the silverware and napkins. It seemed safer that way. True, the napkins drooped a bit, resembling water-lilies in the last stages of dissolution, but no one was going to be in a critical mood after this Board meeting if, indeed, they noticed anything at all.

Meanwhile, I found I had a worse awkwardness to deal with. Both nominees for the so forcibly vacated Director's seat were prowling the corridor outside, trying to look as though they were not waiting for a summons to the Boardroom. They kept passing the kitchen door and I could hear the occasional scraps of conversation between them.

Aldo was disposed to be friendly, but Roddy could not decide whether his dignity and possible about-to-be-exalted position would be impinged by fraternizing with the enemy. On the other hand, Ongar Manganian might win and Aldo would ascend to the Boardroom heights, in which case it would not be safe to have shown open enmity. It made for a very scrappy, nervous interchange of remarks on the weather, the state of the country, or anything except what was going on in the Boardroom.

Inevitably, the kitchen became a neutral refuge for them.

"Hello, everything all right here?" Roddy had been the first to utilize it as a temporary bolt-hole. After all, he could disappear into the Gents only so many times before it would begin to look as though he were either in a state of extreme terror or had something seriously wrong with him.

"Just fine," I said with a sinking heart as he leaned against the door jamb, obviously prepared to stay for a while. From that vantage point, he had a clear view of the corridor by just turning his head slightly.

"Fine, fine," he said vaguely. "Everything looks—and smells—very good. But then, it always is. You do a very good job."

"Thank you." I knew he wasn't really listening, either to what he was saying or to my replies. All his attention was concentrated on the closed door at the end of the corridor.

"Yes. Er . . . excuse me. I think I hear . . ." His voice trailed off as he disappeared from view.

"Something is wrong?" Gretel frowned at the abrupt exit and looked around guiltily to see what new mistake she had made. "He is displeased?"

"He has troubles of his own," I said. "Hello, Mr. Uccello."

Box and Cox. One went out, the other came in.

"Aldo, please," he said. "I'm not the formal type—and I don't believe you are, either." He lounged in the spot just vacated by Roddy, giving a more superficial impression of being at ease, but I noticed that his attention was equally attuned to the happenings at the far end of the corridor.

"Everything looks good—" he gave a perfunctory glance round—"and smells good."

It seemed to be the only thing anyone could think of to say around a kitchen. I'd have expected a more original comment from him, if his parents genuinely ran a restaurant of their own. I suddenly remembered that he had also said that he had a brother who was an electronics wizard and he had started out that way himself. Electronics—electricity, the two were very close, weren't they? Had he been in the building last week? I hadn't seen him then, the first time I had seen him was at the reception with Ongar Manganian— and that reminded me of something else.

"Perhaps you'd like to taste everything," I said. "Just to be sure."

"You caught that, did you?" He was amused. "I thought you did. You looked quite shocked for a moment—before you pulled yourself together."

"It *was* a shock," I said. "I couldn't believe my eyes. It's—it's so archaic! How could you?"

"Oh, I don't mind humouring the old boy." He shrugged. "He imagines he has enemies everywhere. Mind you, he probably has. I'm not saying I'd be happy playing his little game in some corners of the world, but it's probably quite safe here in England."

"Probably..." I let the word trail off. No one could ever be certain about anything concerning Ongar Manganian.

"And I'm safer than most," he said firmly. "Don't forget, I've been familiar with all sorts of flavourings and spices since childhood. If there was anything off about any dish, I'm far better able to spot it than most."

"Just the same ... in this day and age ..."

"People don't change that much," he said. "There's never been a time when certain types wouldn't act to get someone out of the way."

Was he speaking from experience? Suddenly, graphically, the picture of Mark Avery rose in my mind. Mark—sprawled on the carpet—out of someone's way for good. I felt myself sway, my eyes closed ...

"Here, sit down." He moved quickly, pushing the kitchen stool under me. "I'm sorry, I shouldn't have said that. I wasn't thinking. You found him, of course."

"Along with Edda," I said. "She was there first, but she fainted, and then I came along."

"Edda, yes," he said thoughtfully.

"Have a drink of water." Sidonie thrust a glass at me. Gretel watched anxiously.

"I'm all right." I drank some water, then handed the glass back to Sidonie and slid off the stool. The memory of last week was still so strong that I reached out my hand and flipped the light switch on and off in a sort of nervous twitch just to make sure that the electricity was still working. It was.

"Lightning doesn't strike twice in the same place." Sidonie was trying to be encouraging. I smiled wanly.

"The police don't believe it was lightning," I reminded her.

"Furthermore, the belief is a popular fallacy. I myself have seen lightning strike again and again in the same spot." Ongar Manganian stood in the doorway behind me. He had come down the corridor silently. "Not always during the same storm, it is true. But one storm follows another and some places seem to have a fatal attraction for the bolts. They are the magnets in the electromagnetic field." He spoke with authority. How much else did he know about the subject?

Gretel whimpered and stepped back.

"That is right." He looked at her impassively. "It is best not to stand near such a place. Not if you value your safety. Of course—" he turned his head to encompass Aldo— "some people like to live dangerously."

"Is the meeting over?" Aldo met his eyes with equal impassivity. "That didn't take long."

"Not over, no." Ongar Manganian shook his massive head. "Suspended, temporarily, for what they call a corridor conference. Tristram Quardon confers with his minion and—" he jerked his head towards the corridor—"I wish to confer with you."

"Charmingly phrased," Aldo murmured. "Obviously an offer I can't refuse."

"You would be wise not to. If you will excuse us—" He

sketched a bow. "Much as I regret leaving you lovely ladies—"

Gretel cringed another step backwards, smiling nervously. The movement left Ongar Manganian with a clear view of the working counter. His gaze roved over it automatically—it was the food he regretted leaving, not us—and he stiffened suddenly.

"What are you doing with *that*?" he demanded. "Who sent you?" He whirled to face me. "What are you doing here?"

"We're doing the lunches." I looked at him blankly. "We always do. You know that."

"Lunches—hah!" He swooped past me, snatching up something on the counter. "You lie! Who has subverted you? Whose pay are you in? Tell me! I will find out anyway!"

Gretel cowered against the farther wall, taking deep sobbing breaths, hands half hiding her face. I hoped she didn't think our business luncheons usually proceeded along those lines.

"I don't know what you're talking about," I said flatly. In the doorway behind me, help was at hand in case Ongar Manganian passed from merely raving to outright homicidal. Tristram Quardon, Roddy Bletchley, Edda Price and a good selection of the Board were crowding the doorway, drawn by the shouting.

"This! This!" He was shaking something under my nose, his hand such a blur I could not see what he was holding, what had enraged him so. "How do you explain this? What are you doing with a garotte? For whom was it destined?"

"Ongar—" Aldo said softly, warningly. "Ongar, take it easy. What have you got there?" He reached out and stopped the fist in mid-shake. The shape in it began to take form.

"The cheese wire," I said, looking at the coil of wire with a handle at each end. "We're having a cheese board instead of a sweet this afternoon. That's only the cheese wire to cut the cheese smoothly. What's the—'' I broke off.

What's the matter with him? was not a tactful question.

"Cheese wire?" Ongar Manganian repeated wonderingly. He looked down at the object in his hand, examining it as though he had never seen such a thing before. Perhaps they didn't have them in the parts of the world he normally frequented. "Cheese wire?"

"Cheese wire," Aldo said firmly. "You hold one end down, straighten the wire and pull it through the cheese." He tried to take it away from his employer to demonstrate, but Ongar Manganian held on to it stubbornly.

"Cheese wire?" He was still incredulous. "Where I come from, it is a garotte. Ready-made. Ready for—"

"In England," I said, as firmly as Aldo, "this is a cheese wire. You can buy it in any kitchen equipment shop for less than a pound."

"In England!" He shook his head. "Only in England would they dare!" In a swift, serpentine movement, he shook out the wire, uncoiling it, one handle in each hand. "Less than a pound! A deadly weapon: secret, silent, infallible and so cheap. Less than a pound—available at your friendly kitchen equipment shop. Only in England could this be possible!"

"It's a cheese wire," I insisted. "Let me show you—" I reached out for it.

"Let *me* show *you*!" Suddenly, the wire looped around my neck and was drawn snug, but not too tight . . . yet. A wire noose that could cut through the soft flesh as easily as through the yielding cheese. It could cut my head off. I caught my breath and stood silent, not daring to move.

For that terrifying endless moment, no one dared move.

Ongar Manganian's face swung close to mine, his eyes burning, hypnotic. "So easy," he said. "Silent as a knife, final as a bullet—and so disposable. At such a price, anyone can afford to murder. To strike and move away, leaving the garotte embedded in the throat—'' The wire began to tighten.

"All right, Ongar, that's enough." Aldo touched him on the shoulder. "You've made your point."

"Cheese wire!" Abruptly, Ongar Manganian chuckled. "To cut the cheese!" He released his hold at one end and the taut wire relaxed. With one quick—expert—flick of his wrist, he pulled it free and tossed it away from him, back on to the counter where it re-coiled like a waiting snake.

The group in the doorway melted away like witnesses at the scene of an accident fearful of being asked for their names and addresses. I found I was breathing deeply, unable to look at anyone.

"You wanted to talk to me." Aldo led Ongar Manganian from the room. There was a further relaxation in the atmosphere without his presence.

"He is mad!" Gretel sobbed. "Insane! It is not safe to have someone like that abroad in the streets!"

"He's paranoiac, certainly." Sidonie tried for a dispassionate assessment, but she was pale. "He thinks the whole world is plotting against him. I've heard of people like that—" She shuddered, her precocious maturity slipping away. "I've never seen one before. Not in action. Are you all right, Jean! Are you sure you're all right? He looked so—so *mad*."

"That is what I said." Gretel dabbed at her eyes, recovering now that a second opinion endorsed her own. "He is mad!"

"I'm fine." I fingered my throat uncertainly. It seemed that I could still feel that wire tightening around it but, so far as I could tell, there was not even the faintest indentation to mark the spot where it had been.

"Are you all right?" Roddy Bletchley echoed the question from the doorway.

"Fine, thank you," I repeated automatically.

"You weren't frightened, were you?" He came into the room, trying to appear cool and in control of the situation, but tiny beads of perspiration bedabbled his forehead. "We wouldn't have let anything happen. I was all prepared to step in—'' He pulled out his handkerchief and mopped his brow.

"Fine." There must be something else I could say. I turned away, busying myself at the stove. "I'm quite all right."

"The man was out of control!" Mop, mop, mop, but his forehead was still damp. "I've never seen anything like it. He's a danger to the civilized community."

"That is what I say!" Gretel moved forward eagerly. "He is mad! He should be shut away!"

"Er . . . yes," Roddy agreed uneasily. He seemed to be recollecting that, mad or not, Ongar Manganian was allied with Quardon International now and anything that happened to him might rebound on them. "He got carried away for a minute, that's all. Foreigners . . ." He trailed off, belatedly recognizing that Gretel had an accent herself.

"They've gone back to the meeting, have they?" I brought the conversation back to a businesslike level.

"Yes, yes," he said. "It shouldn't be much longer now."

"Just a question of a rubber stamp at this point," Aldo agreed, appearing in the doorway.

Did he sound too happy about it? Roddy shot him a suspicious look.

"You handled that very well." Aldo turned to me. "The old boy was most impressed."

"I didn't do anything," I said. "I was too stunned to move."

"But you didn't show fear. That's the main thing. He has his little ways of testing people. You needn't worry, he'll never try anything like that again. You've passed the test, you're in his good books now."

"Well, he isn't in mine." I turned away to see to the greens. "I can do without that sort of nonsense."

"It won't happen again."

"It shouldn't have happened the first time!" Roddy took up the cudgels on my behalf. I'd have been more impressed if he'd taken them up when Ongar Manganian had the wire around my neck. "The man's a savage. Unfit for civilized life."

"He had to claw his way up out of the gutter." Aldo's face hardened, his eyes were flint; he looked as though he might have done some clawing himself. "It's all right for people who've always lived off the fat of the land to criticize, but you don't get very far if you try to keep to civilized rules where he came from. Once you've escaped, you can begin to learn the niceties of social life."

"I haven't had that sheltered a life," Roddy protested. He tried to look tough, but only succeeded in looking as though he hadn't a claw to his name. He was a fixer, not a fighter; that was why he was so useful to Tristram Quardon.

"Comparatively speaking, you're bound to have had." Aldo, too, was useful to his master, in his own way. Also, it seemed, loyal.

Which one was going to be rewarded by a seat on the Board?

The door at the far end of the hall opened and they both went silent, ending what had threatened to degenerate into a childlike squabble. They waited for the summons.

"Oh dear." Edda Price came into the kitchen, looking quite dazed. "They asked me to tell you. They'll be ready for lunch in about half an hour. They're only going to have a quick drink first." She rubbed her forehead. "I've got to get back. I'm going to have a drink, too. I need one."

Aldo moved forward as though to open a door that was already open. She started and looked at him, then at Roddy... almost guiltily.

"Come on, Edda," I said. "Put them out of their misery. Who's the new Board member?"

"Oh dear!" She darted through the doorway into the safety of the corridor before turning to answer. "It was all so confusing. No one could seem to agree. They went on and on. Then Mr. Manganian suggested a compromise candidate and—" She stopped and gulped.

"And—?" I prompted.

"And . . . well . . . they decided on *me*." She turned and vanished, leaving a thundering silence behind her.

"Yes, I can see it," Aldo said slowly. "It's a clever move. He's off to the States and Womens' Lib is riding high there. It will be to his advantage to say that he's just appointed a woman to the Board. He thinks of every angle."

"You're taking it very calmly, I must say." Roddy wasn't doing so badly himself. The reason became apparent as he continued musing aloud. "Of course, it won't be for too long. She must be coming up to retirement soon—"

"Old directors don't retire as early as the staff." Aldo was amused. "They're beyond the level where the rules apply. I wouldn't be too sure you'll get rid of her so easily. She's got a lot of expertise. It was a good choice."

"Yes. Oh yes!" Roddy seemed to decide that enthusiasm was his best line. "I couldn't be more pleased—" He broke off, perhaps realizing that that was going too far. He'd have been a lot more pleased if he'd got on to the Board himself.

"We ought to go along and offer our congratulations," Aldo said. "Join in the festive drink. It might look a little pointed if we didn't. We wouldn't want to be thought poor losers, would we?"

"No, no, never." Roddy followed him from the room.

"I think it's marvellous," Sidonie said firmly. "Edda should have gone on to the Board long ago. Mark and Tristram both wanted her to, but she had this silly idea that she shouldn't rise too far above her husband. As though he was going to do any rising at all! All he ever wanted was a nice comfortable invalid's life and she let it hold her back."

It was odd to be occasionally reminded that both Sidonie and Lexie knew more about Quardon than I did. Because I was working there first, I tended to forget—and they never stressed—the family links that both of them possessed with Tristram Quardon.

"I'm glad it's happened at last," I said. "It's a shame

Mark Avery couldn't be here to see it—" Too late I remembered that, if Mark Avery were still here, it wouldn't have happened.

I wasn't the only one to remember that. The thought stopped all conversation abruptly and we turned silently to our tasks. . . .

The Directors were soon assembling in the dining-room and there was no more time for idle chatter anyway. I still deemed it safer to leave Gretel in the kitchen doing the preliminary dishing up rather than the actual serving, so Sidonie and I kept busy dashing in and out with loaded trays.

The meal went quickly, conversation was subdued and no one seemed disposed to linger over food. I received a congratulatory nod from Ongar Manganian as he discovered the oysters in the pie, but no one else noticed.

During this time, Gretel appeared to be in a state of increasing agitation. I began to wonder if the pressure was too much for her and whether she would last through the luncheon. Several times she seemed close to tears.

It was not until the end of the meal that I discovered what was wrong. Sidonie had gone ahead, carrying the basket filled with water biscuits, cream crackers, bran and wheat biscuits and oatcakes and I picked up the cheese board to follow her. Then I halted and looked around.

"I am sorry," Gretel sobbed. "I have lost it. Everything was going so well and now it is ruined. You will never take me with you again. I have looked everywhere but I cannot find it. Oh—" Her voice rose in a wail. I hoped the Directors couldn't hear her.

"Never mind," I said. "Never mind that now. Quick, give me a knife!" I snatched a knife from her and hurried towards the dining-room, trying to keep possible implications out of my mind.

The cheese wire-garotte was missing.

Chapter
11

After the Directors had departed, we turned the kitchen upside down, but there was still no trace of the cheese wire.

"Perhaps someone thought it was too dangerous to leave around," I suggested, "and impounded it." I thought of the crowd scene in the doorway as Ongar Manganian had given his little performance with myself as his unwilling assistant. Everyone had been standing there . . . watching. Had it given anyone ideas?

Perhaps someone had taken it for future use. The use Ongar Manganian had so ably demonstrated.

We looked at each other without comment and returned to our search with renewed vigour, but without success. The cheese wire had not fallen behind any of the appliances, had not been tidied away in an unthinking moment into one of the cupboards, nor been absent-mindedly placed at the back of the fridge or stove. The cheese wire had definitely gone missing.

The next time anyone saw it, it might be embedded in someone's throat. The throat of one of the people who had been present today as its possible alternative function had been so vividly demonstrated.

Edda! I saw again that brief flash in Aldo's eyes before he smiled. Fury... or comprehension? The realization that his master had pointed out the method and the weapon for removing the next obstacle from their path. Edda, the compromise candidate, who wasn't expected to occupy the seat on the Board for long.

"It is not here—" Gretel looked up in despair. As a last desperate resort, she had burrowed to the bottom of the waste bin. "It is not anywhere. I have lost it!"

"It's not your fault," I said. I did not add whose fault I thought it was. "Come on, we can't waste any more time looking for it. Let's get back to Notting Hill Gate."

"But," Gretel protested, "we cannot go away and leave it unaccounted for. It—it is a dangerous weapon."

"So is practically anything, if used in the wrong way: the kitchen knives, a gas oven, kebab skewers—" I stopped, reluctant to carry the thought through. *An electric razor.*

"Besides," I added, "anyone can buy a cheese wire. They needn't steal ours. It isn't like buying a gun or poison; the sales person wouldn't even notice." They were also readily available to anyone who had access to a kitchen, especially a restaurant kitchen. The thought cheered me. Aldo had no need to steal ours—unless he had sentimental principles against using family utensils for murder. If he did, he was one of the few; most murders happened in families.

"Go on," Sidonie urged. "What else were you thinking just then? There was a very interesting expression on your face. A penny for them—"

"They're worth more than that," I said. If I uttered what I had just been thinking about Aldo, it would be slander of the most serious sort. Actionable in the High Court, where it could cost me a pretty penny for those thoughts.

"Is everything all right?" Roddy Bletchley stood in the doorway. "I—I mean—" He recoiled before our combined gaze. "You're usually gone by now. I came up to get some papers Tris left in the Boardroom . . . Well, I only thought I'd ask,'' he finished limply.

Send for Roddy. Roddy the Fixer. Could he fix this?

"I'm glad you did," I said, choosing my words carefully. "I'm not sure whether everything is all right or not. I rather fear not. Our cheese wire is missing."

"Missing?" Roddy recoiled even farther, looking as though it would be the last time he ever asked us if everything was all right. "Are you sure?"

"Positive," Gretel said, in a tone that brooked no doubt. "It was here earlier when—when—we all saw it."

"Yes." Roddy blinked, obviously seeing the same thing the rest of us were seeing: the cheese wire tightening around my neck in Ongar Manganian's hands.

"He tossed it on to the counter." I found myself imitating the expert dismissive flick of the wrist. "But when we went to put it on the cheese board, it was gone."

"I noticed you weren't using it," Roddy said. "But I thought you didn't want to bring it to his attention again, not knowing what he'd do. The man's unstable. He must have taken it again and—" He broke off, looking ill.

"*Someone* took it, I'm afraid." That was as far as I was prepared to commit myself.

"He's left the building," Roddy said. "I don't know what we can do about it now." He sounded relieved. Perhaps he thought I'd insist that he face Ongar Manganian to demand the return of the cheese wire.

"Uccello's driving him to Heathrow to catch the New York flight," Roddy continued. "It's quite brilliant, really," he added thoughtfully. "He'll be able to walk on carrying an offensive weapon and no one will ever know. A little bit of wire like that won't show up on the metal detectors the way a knife or gun would. It probably wouldn't register any more than a foil-wrapped packet of aspirins. He'll be able to land in New York all equipped and unsuspected."

"Equipped for what?" I asked. Roddy was letting his imagination—and his dislike for Ongar Manganian—run away with him. "At that level, they don't need to do their own killing."

"No, no, I suppose not." Roddy abandoned the idea reluctantly.

"It's more likely to be used around here." I underlined it for him. "So just keep your eyes open."

"You don't mean—?" He went a pale green. "You don't think—?"

"Just keep your eyes open," I repeated.

The house was empty when we got back. My first surprise gave way to the realization that Mona had been in a mood to drag Nick forcibly into the West End for the afternoon to choose wallpaper and paint as he had promised. They would not have left Lexie and Humpty alone with all the food, so those two must have left earlier.

"I suppose we ought to do the dishes," Sidonie decided regretfully. Everything else seemed to have been taken care of before the others left.

"That's all right," I said. "I'll do them. You two can run along now."

"We're in no hurry." Sidonie began stacking the dishes in the dishwasher. "It isn't fair to dash off and leave you with all the dirty work."

"That's right." Gretel moved impulsively to join her, knocking a pan off the edge of the sink as she did so.

Sidonie and I exchanged glances as Gretel stooped to retrieve the pan. At least it hadn't been something breakable and the pan was a good heavy duty one; it wasn't even dented.

But it wasn't a good idea to let Gretel help with the dishes, no matter how willing she might be. I cast about frantically for an alternative occupation to suggest.

"Jean," Sidonie said hesitantly, interrupting my own thoughts, "you *are* pleased, aren't you?"

"Pleased?" I echoed, watching Gretel move purposefully towards a rack of glasses Mona had left draining on the sinkboard. She was plainly determined to polish them and return them to their cupboard shelf. No prospect could have been less pleasing.

"About the Charity Ball? I thought you would be. You ... you don't *mind* my going ahead and setting it up without consulting you first? I didn't want to disappoint you, in case I couldn't bring it off."

"Oh, Sidonie!" I realized guiltily that I had not thanked her properly. In fact, I hadn't referred to the matter all day. Of course, there had been other things to worry about and I had forgotten it. And all this while, poor Sidonie had been brooding over my lack of response.

"I'm delighted. Really, I am. There just hasn't been time to settle to discussing it properly."

"And you're not upset because—?" She was looking slightly more mollified. "Well, because Lexie and I will have to be on the other side of the table instead of helping you with the serving?"

"Good heavens, no!" Such a thing had never occurred to me. "Of course, you'll be out front with your friends—"

"*I* will help you behind the table," Gretel said proudly. "Now I am getting good experience, you may not need more people."

Sidonie and I exchanged thoughtful glances. "It's true," Sidonie said. "There'll be you and Mona and Nick and Gretel. Since it will be a buffet, four of you ought to be enough." She sounded relieved. "It will mostly be a case of keeping the serving dishes filled and seeing that everything is going smoothly. Perhaps, if you got really pushed, I could slide behind once in a while and—"

"No, I'm sure we'll be able to manage," I said. "It will be *your* night. You just concentrate on having fun."

"Ye-es." She sounded dubious and I remembered that Lexie was going to be at the ball as well. I wondered again just how much fun Sidonie was able to have with Lexie always around, always more vivacious, always ready to deflect the attention of any male. I had seen it happen at some of our luncheons. A man might start out talking to Sidonie, but before either of them realized what was happening, he wound up in conversation with Lexie. It was as well that Sidonie was so sweet-natured, and also that she had other assets—such as a large inheritance due to her from a legacy when she became twenty-one. A fact Lexie was not above hurling at her during one of their infrequent quarrels, as though it were somehow derogatory. Sidonie always reacted as abjectly as though it had been.

And yet, it was Sidonie who paid the rent for the flat they shared. If Lexie thought everyone wasn't aware of that, she was deluding herself. I also suspected that, when they went on their shopping expeditions, Sidonie wound up paying for most of Lexie's clothes . . .

A car door slammed outside, abruptly derailing my train of thought. The noise was followed almost immediately by clatter and commotion at the back door, then Nick and Mona burst into the kitchen carrying rolls of wallpaper, buckets, brushes and boxes of paste.

"There you are—" Nick greeted us. "Or almost all of you. Isn't it lucky we don't have any luncheons scheduled for the next two days? All hands to the pump and we can have this job just about finished by then. It will make a nice break for you from all that cooking."

"*If* you wouldn't mind, that is." Mona was more cautious but equally enthusiastic. The prospect of finishing another room had brightened her eyes and lightened her steps. The idea of having a couple of days free from cooking wasn't doing her any harm either. She looked years younger.

"We will help, *ja*!" Gretel's eyes gleamed. "I *love* the paste and paint—nearly as much as cooking!"

I choked back a laugh at Nick's expression. What it would mean to have Gretel stumbling among the paint pots had obviously not occurred to him before. He would not have spoken so quickly or so carelessly if it had.

"Well . . ." Mona shot Nick an anxious glance. "We'll

see, Gretel. We'll have to be very careful. This is very expensive wallpaper."

"Nothing but the best for our home," Nick said, perhaps too quickly. Mona didn't notice, but I had known him long enough to know that it was suspicious. He was up to something . . . again.

"I will be very careful," Gretel promised. "And," she sighed, "Sidonie is always careful."

Which left Lexie. She might be perfectly willing to help out in an extra-curricular activity, or she might be quite caustic about it. That would depend on whether she was still sulking over her slapped wrist.

"We could start in the withdrawing-room, I suppose." Mona was still considering the earlier problem. "We could practise in there and get into the swing of things before we begin on the dining-room."

"Oh, I don't think we need to bother about the withdrawing-room." Nick was elaborately casual. "It isn't important whether we get that done up."

"Why not?" This time he had aroused Mona's suspicions. The withdrawing-room was at the far end of the dining-room and had once been used as a small parlour to which the ladies could withdraw while the gentlemen passed round port and cigars. Mona had long wanted it as a morning-room for herself, despite the fact that a later occupant of the house had demolished the wall separating the two rooms and replaced it with sliding doors so that the withdrawing-room was an extension of the dining-room. Mona had ambitions to rebuild the inside wall, but it would be some time before they had enough money for a luxury like that.

"Well . . . we won't be needing it immediately. . . ." Nick was obviously aware that he was treading on dangerous ground. He was treading on her dreams—and he had already trampled over too many of them.

"How do you know? We might book a big party straightaway. We'd need to use it as an extension then. Of course it should be done up—and to match the dining-room.''

"Our first bookings won't be for big parties,'' Nick said confidently. Too confidently. "I promise you.''

"I see,'' Mona said evenly, beginning to get the picture. "Then suppose you tell me what our first bookings *will* be. You've already made them, haven't you?''

"Why don't you girls—'' Nick glanced uneasily at Gretel and Sidonie—"take this stuff through into the dining-room? We'll be along in a minute.''

"*Haven't* you?'' It was just short of a scream.

Sidonie and Gretel gathered up rolls of wallpaper and hurried from the kitchen. They had no wish to be involved in a family scene. I felt like going with them, but I had to know the answer to Mona's question myself. I stayed.

"It was while I was having a few drinks with the old chums at the Agency the other week,'' Nick began, with every appearance of frankness. "The subject happened to come up. They've bagged a new account: introducing a range of gourmet foods. The cupboard store type; no tins, no freezing, just the special foil packets with extra-long shelf life. They're going to pull out all the stops on this one—'' His voice was rising enthusiastically. "Top billings, sky-high budget, television ads, poster campaign, double-page spreads in all the glossies and Sunday supplements—''

"And where do we come in?'' Mona asked coldly. "I presume we *do* come in somewhere—or have they offered you your. old job back?''

Nick winced at the low blow, but Mona was right. Nick would not have been so enthusiastic if he had not found a way to deal himself in on it. I began to have a glimmering of what was coming.

"We got to discussing the shooting—'' Nick went on resolutely. Having started, he was going to have to tell her the whole story. "They wanted something better than the usual studio set-up, something on a long-term basis since, if everything goes well, they'll have to film several series of commercials over the next few years—''

"The dining-room," Mona said flatly.

"It's perfect. Plenty of space, the french windows opening out into the garden, the chandelier, the big rosewood table. Best of all, they can set up the cameras in the extension and do fourth-wall shooting from there without any crowding."

"My dining-room," Mona said. "In my home. Splashed over every hoarding, in every magazine I pick up, on everyone's television set. You've given away my privacy!"

"*Our* dining-room," Nick corrected. "*Our* home. And I haven't given anything away. They're paying rather well for the privilege."

"Yes," Mona said. "I wondered why you were being so generous in the shop. You were positively urging me on to choose the most expensive wallpaper. I thought you were trying to impress the sales clerk, but that wasn't it, was it? It was because you weren't paying for it yourself. The Agency has bought my wallpaper and paint!"

"Of course." Nick seemed surprised that she could ever have doubted it. "They wanted the place to look opulent. I told them to leave it to us." He gave her a crafty smile. "Once we get the papering and painting out of the way, we'll talk to them about a carpet."

It was the wrong thing to say. Even Sidonie and Gretel, who had returned to hover in the doorway, knew it.

"We will say good-night now," Gretel said firmly. She took Sidonie by the elbow and began backing away.

"See you first thing in the morning," Nick called after them. "We've got a busy day ahead of us tomorrow."

"Oh yes," Mona said. "We're in a rush, aren't we? How soon does the filming start?"

"Plenty of time," Nick said serenely. "A couple of weeks. We'll have the work all done and the paint dry before then. It will work out perfectly."

"Oh, perfect," Mona said. "Perfect! Everything is perfect for you—as long as someone else is paying for it!"

"I don't know what you're upset about. You know we couldn't have afforded this on our own. Perhaps not for years. You're the one who's always on about getting this place finished."

"But I wanted it for ourselves. Not for everyone who feels like coming in and using it as their own. Not for your film crews, not for your old buddies—not even for your sister and her apprentices. I wanted it for *us*!"

She burst into tears and rushed from the room. We heard her stumble on the stairs and I started forward.

"Better not." Nick caught my arm. "It didn't sound as though you were particularly in her good graces either. Just leave her alone. She'll come round, she always does."

"Some day you're going to push her too far," I warned him.

"I doubt it," he said. "But we'll let her cool down for a few days before I tell her the rest of my plans."

"The rest? Oh no, Nick! What else have you done?"

Upstairs, the bedroom door slammed. Nick winced.

"I haven't done anything else . . . yet." He gave me a cheeky grin. "It's just a brilliant idea in the back of my mind. When the crew gets here and they see the kitchen—"

"Not the kitchen, Nick!" For a moment, I felt murderous. All my sympathies shifted over to Mona. "We *need* the kitchen for cooking. *That's* our livelihood. We can't have film crews and actors underfoot there."

"Not actors," Nick said. "That's the beauty of it. Just Mona."

"Mona?"

"She's a good-looking woman. You may not have noticed it, but she is. With just enough maturity to inspire confidence in consumers. And the way she handles the food and equipment: that sureness of touch, the no-nonsense way she can decapitate a carrot. They'll love her. A few subtle words in the ear of the director and producer, and you wait and see. They'll have her dishing up the sponsor's product in no time."

"Oh no. You'll never be able to talk her into that one."

"And no reason why it should stop there," he went on dreamily. "She'd be a sensation in her own cooking series, using her own recipes. I can see it all—" He stretched out a hand, unrolling glorious future. "Today, dunking the new product in boiling water; tomorrow, the new Fanny Cradock!"

"But you're no Johnnie! She'll never do it. She'll see you in hell first!"

"Don't bet on it," he said smugly. "She's putty in my hands. Just let me work around to it in my own time and my own way. You'll see. And then you can call me Svengali."

"I wouldn't dream of it," I said. "If Svengali had only had your nerve, he'd have been Emperor of Europe."

Chapter
12

It was more than a week before Mona began to thaw out and return to a state approximating pleasant. During this time, Nick walked on eggshells and acted the part of the model husband. He stayed close to home, never suggested dropping down to have a drink with the boys, and gave no indication that he had any plans for the future beyond getting the dining-room into the best possible order.

It was too much to hope that he had abandoned his idea. The occasional glint in his eyes as he surveyed a particularly photogenic moment in the kitchen (Mona removing a tray of muffins from the oven; Mona stirring a steaming cauldron of soup and testing the flavour by tilting the hollow-handled wooden spoon so that the soup ran down from the large bowl at the stirring end to the small sipping bowl in her hand) betrayed him.

All the world's a stage. And Nick was more than willing—he was eager—to turn his entire home into one great big stage-set.

Some women would have relished the prospect. Lexie would have revelled in it. But Mona was a private person by nature and she had been raised in the old-fashioned tradition: a lady gets her name in the newspapers on only three occasions in her life; when she is born, when she married and when she dies. Anything more was vulgar and ostentatious.

Mona cherished her privacy; she wanted her home and her life to belong to herself—and Nick. Now Nick was destroying the privacy of their home. Just wait until she discovered that he planned to strip away her personal privacy and turn her into a public figure! I wouldn't be surprised if she sprinkled ground glass over the crunchy breadcrumbs and chopped almonds of his apricot crumble some night. I wasn't sure I'd blame her if she did.

Meanwhile, the dining-room was nearly finished. Nick had done the ceiling first, inexpertly and by himself, but it hadn't looked too bad after the second coat. The rest of us took turns painting the woodwork, alternating with the necessary chores in the kitchen. Sidonie had worked with her usual calm competence, although her heart was obviously in the kitchen. Lexie had been surprisingly cooperative and cheerful, if a bit slapdash. Gretel had amazed us all.

For the first time, we had discovered something Gretel could do without constantly putting her foot wrong. She handled paintbrushes with ease, almost with skill; but it was when we reached the delicate task of matching and hanging strips of wallpaper that she really came into her own. She scampered up and down the stepladder, patiently adjusting the long strip of wallpaper by fractions of an inch until the pattern matched so exactly we could not see the join after we stuck it down. She was laughing and exultant when she realized she could do something better than the rest of us.

Unfortuantely, *her* heart was still in the kitchen, too.

"I have been finding some wonderful old English cookbooks in the Portobello Road markets," she confided to me. "You must come to dinner, Jean, and let me show you. Such recipes you never have seen!"

That was what I was afraid of. Some English cookbooks, even in recent times, had been published with deadly errors in them. Every now and again one saw a desperate plea from a publisher asking for the return of all copies of a certain cookbook and added that, if you did not wish to return the book and receive another, for God's sake, do not attempt the recipe on page such-and-such.

Most recently, an enterprising cookery writer (who clearly did not test all her recipes or the publication would have been posthumous) had included a recipe for a delicious dish of cooked rhubarb leaves—the part you normally throw away. (*Why just cook the rhubarb stalks and waste all those lovely green leaves?* she had asked. "Because they're loaded with deadly oxalic acid and can kill you, that's why," someone had answered.) Erratum slips had gone flying, presumably to good effect, since there had been no subsequent reports of deaths and lawsuits.

I decided it was my duty to have dinner with Gretel and check out those cookbooks. Murphy's Law ruled when Gretel stepped into a kitchen: if anything could go wrong, it would. Getting hold of one of those misprinted cookbooks would be typical of her.

"Just something very light," I had insisted, vestiges of self-preservation clinging to me. "I'll be having a hearty lunch with a prospective client earlier. I couldn't possibly eat much."

"A light supper," Gretel had promised. "That will be easy. You will see."

"It smells delicious," I said as I entered, uncomfortably aware that this might be the only genuine compliment I could bestow during the course of the evening. Gretel's creations often looked and smelled delicious—but, as some sage had observed, the proof of the pudding was in the eating.

"Thank you. Let me take your coat," Gretel said, beaming. "Come and have a drink."

"We moved out of the diminutive hallway into an almost

equally tiny sitting-room with a table and two straight chairs in one corner. "You will have sherry?"

"That will be fine." I sat in an armchair while Gretel carried my coat through to the small bedroom. I had seen her flat before; it was a single flat like thousands of others in London, rebuilt to squeeze too many rooms into too small a space, in not very good repair, and renting for an iniquitous sum. The alternative was a huge mansion flat, shared with several other people—some of them strangers—and renting for a hugely iniquitous sum.

Behind me, I could hear Gretel fussing around in the kitchen, then she reappeared with glasses of sherry and a dish of salted almonds which she set by my elbow.

"There," she said, sitting down. "This is so nice, *ja*?" She looked around with dissatisfaction. "In so small a flat, one should not feel sometimes lonely. Sidonie and Lexie are so lucky to share a flat. They have such fun. And you, in the big house with your family. There is always someone to laugh with."

"Yes," I said doubtfully. There hadn't been many laughs with Nick and Mona lately.

"I have sometimes thought," she confided, "of asking Sidonie and Lexie if they would have room for me. It is such a big flat. Do you think they would mind?"

"I don't think they'd mind your asking," I said cautiously. "But I don't know if they *do* have so much extra room. The flat belongs to Sidonie's family and I think they have to keep a spare bedroom available in case her parents want to stay in town at any time."

"Oh," she sighed. "I was hoping, perhaps, they might like to have another there to help with the bills."

"You can try." I dipped idly into the salted almonds— they seemed to be rather unevenly toasted. "It can't do any harm to ask."

"Perhaps I will try," Gretel said with an air of decision. "As you say, it cannot—What is the matter? Are you all right?"

I couldn't answer, I was choking. I had the feeling that something had exploded in my mouth and was taking the top of my head off. I gagged, choked and managed to expel the contents of my mouth into the tiny paper cocktail napkin Gretel had provided. Then I lay back, gasping for air, eyes watering.

"What is wrong?" Gretel bent over me anxiously. "Is it a fit? Should I call a doctor?"

"Gretel," I said weakly. "Gretel, what did you *do* to those almonds?"

"I do them just the way I learn from you," she said. She paused and sniffed the air as I inhaled and exhaled rapidly several times. "Oh dear . . ."

"Yes," I said, a trifle grimly as I sat up and wiped my eyes, then cautiously opened the paper napkin for a closer inspection. "*Oh dear!*"

"So that is where they went," Gretel said with an air of enlightenment. A mystery had been explained. "I know I have peeled more garlic cloves, but when I go to press them, they are not there."

A peeled garlic clove and a blanched almond; two gleaming white ovals, almost indistinguishable at a quick glance. When you considered Gretel working with both raw materials at the same time, there was an almost fated inevitability about the whole thing.

"I must have dropped some garlic cloves into the almonds when I am placing them in the baking tray." Gretel was still working it out. "So that is why some of them came out a funny colour. I thought it was that the oven did not heat properly."

"Yes," I said. I should have been more careful. Everything Gretel attempted in the culinary line required close inspection before commiting it to the palate.

"Oh, Jean, I am so sorry. Is it awful?"

"It *is* rather ghastly." I sipped at the sherry and made a face. Everything tasted of garlic. "Could I have a glass of water please?"

"Yes, yes!" She dashed to get it. I heard the clink of ice tumbling into a tall glass and wondered wryly if she could manage to ruin *that*.

She had done her best. There were tiny flowers embedded in the centre of the ice cubes. Since they resembled no known blooms, I had to assume they were some plastic fantasy. They looked pretty enough suspended in the ice, but were going to look pretty dispiriting slumped at the bottom of the glass when the ice melted. They were also a trap for any unwary drinker who might drain the glass without due care and attention.

I wasn't going to linger over my drink that long. I gulped it greedily, letting the icy water anaesthetize my taste-buds. Gradually the aftertaste of garlic began to fade.

"You are all right?" Gretel asked anxiously. "I must go now to cook the meal—"

"Please," I said. "No garlic. I've had enough to last me a long while."

"No, no," she assured me. "No garlic. It is mushroom omelette. With herbs. Very delicate flavour—garlic would kill it."

It had nearly killed me, but I allowed myself to relax. The proposed dish sounded harmless, except—

"Where did you get the mushrooms?" I asked cautiously. "You didn't pick them yourself, did you?" With commercially grown mushrooms available at all times in shops, Gretel might not realize that the season for wild mushrooms was between last July and late September. It would be only too like her to have noticed and picked any mushroom-like fungus she had found growing in a park or garden.

"No, no," she laughed. "When would I have the time? Where would I go to do so? No, I buy these in the market early this morning."

I relaxed again. That should be all right. "Is there anything I can do to help?"

"No, no. You sit there and finish your drink. Everything is under control."

If it was, it was the first time. I leaned back and sipped at my sherry again. It tasted less obnoxious this time; almost like sherry, in fact. Another few minutes and my sense of taste might return.

There were clattering sounds from the kitchen, but I forced myself to remain seated. I tried to occupy myself by attempting to identify the various noises emanating from the kitchen.

Crack—that was obviously a knife breaking an egg. *Clack*—that was an empty eggshell hitting the floor. I hoped it was empty.

Butter began sizzling and spitting in the frying-pan while Gretel beat the eggs vigorously enough to chip the bowl. I hoped she hadn't used so much butter it would splatter on to the gas flames and set the frying-pan alight.

There was too much to worry about. The kitchen was fraught with peril when someone like Gretel was working in it.

There was a final explosion of sound: the hiss as the mixture was poured into the hot frying-pan; a long triumphant sigh of relief from Gretel; and then the steady bubbling sound as the mixture settled down and began to cook—too rapidly and at too high a temperature, but a leathery omelette was something I could manage.

"Very soon now—" Gretel whirled back into the room, tossing dishes and cutlery on to the table and setting our places with more enthusiasm than care. She should not have left the omelette unattended, but I didn't feel that I ought to sound too much like an instructor since this was a social visit. Apart from which, I had the fated feeling that nothing was going to save the omelette, anyway.

"Sit there! Sit there!" Gretel protested as I made to get up. "There is nothing you can do. I have done it all."

That was what I was afraid of. I settled back in my chair and tried not to look at the plastic petals beginning to protrude from the melting ice cubes.

I heard the gurgle of wine running into tulip-shaped

glasses, a further jangle of cutlery, then Gretel's footsteps returning to the kitchen. "You can sit up at the table now," she called. "I am coming right in."

I dutifully took my place. Gretel re-entered in a triumphal rush and plonked a heated plate in front of me. I stared down at the food, bemused, trying to think of a polite comment. I had never seen a rigid omelette before.

"It smells delicious." That much, I could manage with perfect truth. I probed delicately at it with a fork—and encountered firm resistance.

Surely she hadn't booby-trapped the omelette with plastic flowers? No, nothing so grand. I probed a little further and dislodged a small twig. After a moment of intensive study, I identified it as something of the dried herb line. I couldn't say what without tasting it and, somehow, I wanted to put off that evil moment.

"Well—" Gretel lifted her glass. "Cheers, you say."

"Cheers," I responded, thinking I could say a lot more than that if I let myself go. But how can you convince someone that she's set her heart on the wrong line of work?

She set down her glass, picked up her fork and dug into her omelette with gusto. I followed her example with a great deal less enthusiasm.

After fighting a fragment of omelette free of the whole, I discovered the reason for its rigidity. The egg coating encased an entire saucer-sized open-cap giant mushroom. While cooked on the outside, the egg mixture that had dribbled into the open gills of the mushroom was still runny. The most charitable thing I could think about Gretel's use of dried herbs was that she had inadvertently spilled a packet into the omelette while working. Surely she couldn't have used that much deliberately?

I looked up and saw Gretel watching me anxiously. There was nothing I could do but smile and try to eat the concoction. It was like trying to munch one's way through a compost heap.

"I'm afraid I'm not very hungry," I murmured, leaving as much as I dared.

"*Ja*." She gave a resigned nod. She had not been able to finish hers either. "Perhaps next time I should cut the mushroom up into small pieces?"

"That would help," I agreed. "Also, perhaps, a lighter hand with the herbs. And use fresh herbs, if possible."

"*Ja*." She sighed and cleared away the plates, then brightened. "Now comes dessert," she announced.

I braced myself.

The refrigerator door opened and shut. There ensued a long silence. Then came a series of clinking sounds and dark Nordic mutterings. I began to grow unnerved.

I bit down a renewed offer of help and crossed to the bookshelves on the other side of the room. I had intended to vet Gretel's choice of cookery books and this seemed as good a time as any. I had the feeling that there was going to be a considerable delay before the next course.

Looking over the miscellany of cookery books ranged along the bookshelves, I realized that Gretel had been speaking loosely when she described them as English cookbooks. They were printed in the English language, but not all of them could be correctly classed as English.

There was the obligatory Mrs. Beeton's—one of the later versions, not featuring the apocryphal "*First, catch your hare*." Which was a shame—I would rather trust Gretel to catch a hare than to cook one.

This edition contained other choice items of shopping advice, however, which gave a fascinating picture of a vanished world of autocratic housewives and long-suffering shopkeepers. I hoped Gretel never attempted to utilize any of these hints; I could not see a modern merchant standing by calmly while his prospective purchaser tested his merchandise for freshness and quality according to Mrs. Beeton:

"*In selecting nutmegs, prick them with a pin; if good, the oil will instantly spread round the puncture.*" . . . "*To choose a ham . . . run a skewer in close to the bone in the middle of the ham.''* . . . *"Dip a bright steel knitting needle into the milk . . .''* . . . *"Plunge a knife into the butter . . .''* . . . *"Macaroni, when good, breaks crisply.''*

I had a brief unsteadying vision of Gretel—or anyone else—rampaging through a shop selecting her purchases according to Mrs. Beeton's recommended methods, pursued by one of today's shopkeepers who object even to a gentle squeeze of a tomato. These days, it's the consumers who are downtrodden.

I replaced Mrs. Beeton and continued along the bookshelf. There was a strange American tome featuring such hackle-raising delicacies as Cranberry-Horseradish Mousse and Peanut Butter Aspic. (On the whole, I was beginning to feel that I had got off lightly with tonight's menu.)

Yet another proclaimed itself "An American Cookbook for India." Entranced, I read its opening homily: *"Finding your cook is the first step towards having good food and serving it well, for your dinners will be no better than the man who makes them."* Oh, that was the right cookbook for Gretel! If there was one thing she needed for perfect meals, it was someone else to cook the food.

She had also unearthed a couple of strange little books about cooking in wartime, so I supposed I could only be thankful that she hadn't tried to feed me Woolton Pie. As it was, one of them strongly advocated something called Hay Box Cookery and gave minute instructions for constructing a hay box, suggesting substitute materials in case the reader could not acquire either asbestos sheeting or hay. Since the substitutes advocated were, respectively, many layers of newspapers and small balls of newspaper, and I had always understood that there was a shortage of newsprint at that time, I replaced the book on the shelf marvelling at the resourcefulness of an earlier generation.

However, the cookbooks Gretel had acquired seemed safe enough. Although some of the recipes struck me as decidedly eccentric, there was nothing in them that could actually kill one. Not even one so unwary as to dine with Gretel.

"Yee-an . . ." A wail of distress came from the kitchen. "Come and help me, please. I am in trouble with my yelly!"

"Coming." She was also in trouble with her "j" which had a tendency to slip under stress. It had taken me some time to grow accustomed to being called Yean, although she was improving lately.

I entered the kitchen to find her struggling with a jelly-mould. Whatever she had put in it seemed determined to stay in it and she was on the verge of tears.

"Wait a minute," I said. She had upended the mould over the serving plate and was shaking it furiously. "You won't get far that way. You want to dip a knife into warm water, dry it, and then run it around the inside of the mould."

"I have tried that already!" She gave the mould another ferocious shake. "It does not work!"

"Then set the mould in warm water for a minute."

"I haff tried that, too. It does not work!"

Too late, I remembered hearing the sound of an electric kettle reaching full steam just before it clicked off. I glanced at a basin from which steam was still rising.

"We'll try again," I said encouragingly. "Keep calm."

"*Ja*." With a sigh of exasperation, she plunged the mould back into the basin of boiling water.

"No, wait a minute—" I rescued the mould and set it down on the table. "Let's try the knife again first."

I dipped the knife, dried it and worked it around the inside of the mould. It seemed to encounter sporadic resistance: perhaps there were lumps of fruit in there? I could not discern through the murk.

"What is it?" I asked, hoping I did not sound too dubious.

"It is called Bavarian Fantasy," Gretel said proudly. "In three layers; lime chiffon, almond cream and raspberry cream." She reached for the mould possessively.

"How ambitious." I let her take the mould with a gloomy

certainty that we were heading for disaster. Gretel always wanted to try the most ambitious recipes when she had not yet conquered the basic principles.

"We try again!" Before I could intervene, she upended the mould over the serving plate again instead of putting the plate on top of the mould and then turning it over.

Plop . . . plop . . . swoosh.

The first two layers fell out separately. The final layer, dissolved by the boiling water in the basin, poured green foam over the other two, flooding the serving dish and slopping over on the table.

"Well, back to the old drawing-board," I muttered.

Gretel said something explosive in her own language. It was probably just as well that I could not translate.

"Never mind." I tried to be soothing. "We just eat the two good layers." But I had fresh qualms as Gretel poured off the green liquid. The remaining jelly seemed curiously immovable. I began to suspect that we were going to have to cut it with a knife—possibly a carving knife.

"Perhaps we'd better dish up here." I picked up the serving spoon and, under the guise of passing it to Gretel, managed to tap it experimentally on the raspberry cream. It bounced off.

"*Ja.*" She attacked the jelly with a vigour that suggested she had made jelly—although not in this particular form—before. The serving spoon cut firmly through the resilient mass.

For a moment, I thought she had won—and then I saw the long stringlike threads clinging to the spoon, like tentacles, as she lifted the jelly and tried to deposit it in a dessert dish.

Gretel gave a wordless cry and hurled the spoon, milk jelly and all to the floor. I could not help thinking that that was the best place for it. But Gretel was genuinely upset, hovering between hysteria and tears.

"Never mind," I said quickly. "How about some cheese and crackers instead?"

She wavered for another perilous moment, then we met each other's eyes.

It was impossible to say which of us giggled first. Suddenly, we both exploded with laughter, the dangerous moment passed and disappeared. We carried cups of coffee back into the living-room and sat down, still giggling weakly.

At some future point, however, I was going to have to suggest to Gretel that she might do better by switching to a career in interior decoration.

Chapter
13

One interesting side-effect of the forthcoming Charity Ball was that Sidonie began to overshadow Lexie for perhaps the first and only time in her life. Neither of them seemed consciously aware of it, but it was happening. Sidonie was more quietly confident, absorbed in committee discussions and arrangements when she wasn't on duty, no longer such a satellite of Lexie's, her own interests becoming paramount.

"Sidders and her stupid old charity work!" Lexie was restive and jeering. "I don't know how she can bother wasting her time like that."

"Mm-hmm," I said absently, spreading pâté on the toast rounds for the Tournedos Rossini. No one would ever have to worry about Lexie wasting time on something that did not benefit her directly.

"But it isn't *fair*," Lexie complained. "Sidders's family have more money than God—and she doesn't even *care*. She's more interested in things like this stupid cooking lark. Catch *me* doing it if I didn't have to!"

"You'd better not let her catch you calling her Sidders," I said. "You know she doesn't like it."

Lexie's declaration did not surprise me. I had always

known her heart wasn't in her cooking—which was rather a shame. She was quite good at it when she paid attention. It was no secret that she would prefer to be a social butterfly, fluttering from one chic restaurant to another, sitting out front consuming delicious meals rather than being back in the kitchen creating them. Unfortunately, like so many of us, she couldn't afford it. That was what she found so rankling about Sidonie's attitude. Even without coming into her inheritance, Sidonie had enough money to lead the sort of life Lexie longed for, but that life didn't attract Sidonie at all. Sidonie was genuinely and increasingly absorbed in her cooking studies and in her work for charity. Perhaps it was the absorption Lexie envied as much as anything. What Lexie needed was a subject of her own she could immerse herself in—or, perhaps, the ability to do so.

"I'm sorry, Jean." Belatedly, Lexie realized that she might have been offensive. "I don't mean there's anything *wrong* with cooking for a living. I'd just rather not, that's all."

"Then you'd better find a rich husband." (As though the idea hadn't been drilled into her from earliest childhood.)

"You sound like my mother." Before, Lexie had just been rebellious, now she turned bitter. "She's always going on about it. But it's not all that easy, you know, not when you don't have any money yourself and everyone knows it. They're all looking for heiresses, even if they *are* rich themselves. Two fortunes are better than one. And if you've got land as well . . ."

She let the thought trail off. The air between us was suddenly electric with rancour. I knew she was thinking of the rich acres of Gloucestershire where Sidonie's family farmed and lived in a Queen Anne manor house. Yet another part of her heritage Sidonie did not appreciate enough, for a small portion of which Lexie would have given her eyeteeth.

Really, from Lexie's point of view, it was hardly surprising that she let Sidonie pay so many of her bills. In some obscure corner of her mind, she must feel that it was owing to her. And when Sidonie came into the bulk of her inheritance and was no longer protected by the Trust Fund . . .

"If only my father had lived—" Lexie was suddenly wistful. "He was brilliant, you know, really he was. Everyone said so. He'd have built up a business of his own—just like Uncle Tris. Bigger. Better. I *know* he would have. But *his* heart was faulty, too—and the doctors didn't know so much about Pacemakers in those days. Uncle Tris was lucky, his trouble didn't develop until much later in life and medical science was so much more advanced. I suppose it's lucky for me, too. If it runs in the family. . ."

Her hand fluttered to her blouse again, but not to undo any button this time. Her fingers slipped between the buttons, pressing against her flesh, testing the beat of a heart that might someday prove treacherous.

"Come on," I said briskly, trying to conceal a sympathy which might send Lexie from an unconscious concern into a full-scale dramatic scene if she noticed it. "The Board meeting will be breaking up any minute now. We don't have time for iffing around."

"All right." Lexie gave a reluctant laugh and shrugged her shoulders dismissively. "My mother married the wrong brother, that's all. Not that she'd have had much of a chance with Uncle Tris—he's married to his business. No woman ever had a chance."

She was certainly right so far as Lady Pamela was concerned. I had seen Tristram Quardon's face once when a telephone call had come through from her when I was in his office. True, no one likes a begging call—and I had the impression Lady Pamela didn't make any other kind, at least not to her wealthy relative—but there seemed to be a more personal dislike behind his cold expression. Edda had told me that one of the main things he disliked about Lady Pamela was the way she had raised his brother's only child—but he had not been fully aware of that until Lexie had decamped on her ill-fated New York escapade.

"There, that's done!" Sidonie came back into the kitchen.

She had been setting round the smoked rainbow trout in the dining-room. The idea was to speed things up when the Directors finally got round to the thought of food by having the first course waiting for them. Edda had suggested it, in the hope of getting them back to work a bit sooner. We doubted it, but were willing to let her try the experiment.

Lexie had been spreading the thinly sliced brown bread with unsalted butter and arranging the triangles on small plates. She held two of the plates out to Sidonie who took them automatically, but paused before returning to the dining-room.

"Has Lexie told you the good news?" she asked.

"No." Nothing Lexie had said so far could possibly be construed as good news. "What is it?"

"I was going to let you tell her," Lexie said. "It's *your* news." She began to butter more bread, although we already had enough.

"My birthday present." Sidonie's face was aglow. "My father is giving me a microwave oven for the flat. Lexie suggested it to him. Isn't it super? And, Jean, he's letting me have it early so we'll be able to use it at the Charity Ball."

"How nice," I said. We could handle the refreshments perfectly well without a microwave oven, but Sidonie was so pleased I hadn't the heart to say anything to dampen her spirits.

"Isn't it?" She beamed. "I'll be able to cook meals for the freezer and then we can have them as soon as we want them, whatever time we come in."

"That was what sold your father on the idea," Lexie said. "He's the one who arrives unexpectedly at all hours. He's just looking after his own comfort."

"Pay no attention to her," I told Sidonie. "It's a lovely birthday present."

"Wait until *next* birthday," Lexie said softly.

Sidonie flushed guiltily and I realized that her next birthday must be the crucial one.

A familiar babble of voices began at the end of the corridor and snapped us all back to attention.

"Here they come," Sidonie said gratefully.

"Not for ages yet," Lexie said. "They're only just out of the meeting. They'll be an hour yet in the bar."

"Take the bread through, anyway, Sidonie," I directed.

Roddy nearly collided with her as she dashed past him. "Is everything all right?" He gave his characteristic territorial call. I could visualize him as one of the not very adventurous feathered species, with drab camouflaging plumage, head ducked low against possible predators, but determined to preserve his nest and nestlings.

"Why shouldn't it be?" Lexie snapped. "Really, Roddy!"

But it had not always been. It had not been so very long since the worst possible thing had happened in this building. Was Lexie so deep in her own concerns that she had forgotten already?

"What's happening with the investigation?" I asked. "What are the police doing now?"

"Nothing." He seemed surprised at the question. "What should they be doing? The Inquest decided it was all a terrible accident. Misadventure. The building had been renovated before Quardon International took it over and someone botched the wiring. At this point in time, no one could even say who the electricians were or whether they're still in business. It must have been some cowboy outfit. Impossible to trace them now. Amazing something didn't happen before. Of course, Mark didn't use that switch a great deal. He usually used a battery-operated razor, but the batteries had worn down so he reverted to the mains razor he kept in his desk for emergencies. It would probably have been all right even then—if he hadn't spilled the water."

"Roddy!" Sidonie returned just in time. I was feeling distinctly queasy and I noticed Lexie had gone a pale green. But Sidonie had not heard the conversation and was intent on her own preoccupations. "Roddy, *you'll* buy a ticket, won't you?"

"What?" Roddy turned, blinking at this sudden distraction. "What ticket?"

"For my Charity Ball," Sidonie said. "Come on, Roddy, it's in a good cause."

"Tell him how much it costs," Lexie jeered. She had regained her colour and was enjoying Roddy's discomfiture.

Sidonie told him and Roddy went green in his turn. "Come on, Roddy," Sidonie said again, while I marvelled silently. Once—and not so long ago—she would never have thrust herself forward like this. Now she advanced on Roddy, gently bullying, brandishing the ticket. "You know you can afford it. Just one ticket—you don't even have to take anyone. Lexie and I will be there and we'll dance with you. Just one ticket—"

"Ticket? Ticket? What is tickets?" Ongar Manganian was suddenly in our midst. I had known he was back in town, but I hadn't been certain that he would be at Quardon today. Just in case, though, I had prepared Tournedos Rossini.

"For my Charity Ball—" Lexie turned to him. "Next week. Would you like one?"

"An English Charity Ball—" Ongar Manganian advanced into the kitchen, Aldo right behind him, and removed the printed card from Sidonie's fingers.

"I was just buying one myself, Mr. Manganian," Roddy said quickly. "It's a very good cause." He fumbled for his chequebook.

"And you think I will enjoy this?" Ongar Manganian brought a fierce gaze to bear on Sidonie.

"I'm sure you will," she said pertly, almost flirtatiously. Perhaps she had been getting more than it seemed out of her association with Lexie; perhaps she had been studying Lexie's methods of handling men. "You see," she added, with the air of one producing an ace of trumps, "Jean is doing the catering."

"Ah!" He gave her an approving nod. "You know your best selling point. You are a clever young lady. It does, indeed, make a difference that Jean is doing the cooking. It is always valuable to know that a trustworthy cook is in charge."

He glanced keenly at Aldo and a silent message seemed to pass between them. "We will have two tickets," he decided.

So he didn't trust me enough to come without his official taster.

"I'm sure Mr. Quardon will want a ticket, too," Roddy said.

"Don't worry." Sidonie was triumphant. "I've already got him. Two tickets! He's bringing Edda Price."

"That is well." Ongar Manganian nodded again. "I have the feeling that she is a lady who could do with more festivity in her life."

"You needn't feel sorry for *her*—" The words seemed torn from Roddy. "She gets what she wants—in her own quiet way."

And now did she want Tristram Quardon? Something in his tone brought that suspicion to mind. But if so, what about that invalid husband lurking in the background? I saw Lexie catch the implication. Her head snapped up and turned briefly in Roddy's direction.

The nuances appeared to have escaped Ongar Manganian. He crossed the room in pursuit of his major interest and began browsing among the saucepans on the stove.

"Ah, asparagus tips," he approved. He had already given a happy smile to the Tournedos Rossini as he passed them. He lifted the lid of another saucepan. "And new potatoes." He replaced the lid and looked around. "And for dessert?"

"In the fridge," I said resignedly. He opened the door with the air of a child trying not to tear too greedily at his stocking on Christmas morning.

"Ah, creme caramel. Excellent! Splendid!" He straightened and beamed down at me. "I shall now join the others for an apéritif in blissful anticipation of the feast awaiting me." Still beaming, he left the room, Aldo following closely at his heels as though to guard him from a sudden stab in the back.

"You certainly know how to please the old boy, Jean." There was an edge to Roddy's voice which made the remark more of an insinuation than a compliment.

"Anything edible would please him," I said and, wanting to retaliate, added, "But what have you been doing since we last saw you? Have you found our cheese wire yet?"

"Cheese wire?" He looked at me blankly, as though I had suddenly lapsed into Sanskrit.

"The garotte," I amended nastily. "The one that went missing from our supplies the last time we were here."

"Oh yes, I remember. The thing that foreign girl kept rabbiting on about. If you ask me, she lost it and was afraid to admit it. Probably let it fall out of the window or something and didn't want to tell you."

"Gretel wouldn't do that," I said.

"No? I notice you don't have her with you today. Got rid of her, have you?"

"Gretel is working with Mona today," I said coldly. "You aren't our only client, you know."

Actually, we had no other assignment today. Gretel and Mona were cooking in anticipation of the first photographic session in the dining-room tomorrow. We were expected to provide all the frills and garnishes for the products they would be photographing. A subdued Gretel had volunteered to remain with Mona today.

I think Gretel was still feeling abashed at her failure to set the perfect meal before me, flawlessly cooked, which she had so obviously planned in her imagination. She now dogged Mona's footsteps, watching every move, as though she might discover the secret of perfect cooking if only she paid close enough attention. I knew that she was beginning to get on Mona's nerves, but everything was getting on Mona's nerves these days. It was safer to leave her with Mona today than to take her along where she might wreak more havoc.

"Poor Gretel," Lexie said. "You shouldn't be so hard on her, Roddy. Just because you've fallen down on your job." There was a challenge in her voice. "Finding the cheese wire, I mean."

"It's nowhere to be found." Roddy almost snapped at her. "I've told you. Either your foreign girl lost it, or someone else—" he glanced over his shoulder—"carried it out of the building with him."

I remembered Roddy's slanderous earlier theory that Ongar Manganian might have taken it to New York for dark purposes of his own. I didn't blame Roddy for being reluctant to repeat it if Ongar Manganian was on the premises and possibly within earshot.

"Here's your ticket, Roddy." Sidonie gave it to him with an air of faint disapproval and stood waiting while he wrote out his cheque.

Chapter
14

Nick was playing with fire again.

Mona had been in a bad mood when we returned to the house yesterday afternoon and she was in a worse mood this morning. It didn't help that the hallway was cluttered with camera and lighting equipment and criss-crossed with cables. Strangers tracked mud through it and into the dining-room. It was as well that the decorating hadn't extended to a carpet or she really would have been hysterical.

As it was, she went about the kitchen tight-lipped, except to snap at Gretel when she found her too close on her heels. Lexie and Sidonie kept well out of her way. Nick was in the dining-room, reliving past glories with his old colleagues and taking bows on his perspicacity in getting out of the rat-race in time and setting himself up in such a thriving new business where he was his own boss.

Of necessity, I was acting as liaison between the dining-room and kitchen. Mona wasn't speaking to Nick, and she wasn't saying very much to me. I knew that Nick had not yet approached her with his ideas for making her rich and famous—and I wasn't looking forward to her reaction when he did.

They were shooting stills for magazine ads today and for the next few sessions. I knew that by the time they were ready to start filming, Nick hoped to have manipulated them into using Mona instead of a professional model. To this end, he had already started making leading remarks.

"I must show you round after we've got this set up," Nick said to the clutch of Directors (Creative, Photographic, Product, Sales and Unidentified) surrounding him. "Wait until you see the kitchen."

I shook my head vehemently at him. Mona had ruled the kitchen out of bounds. If any of them showed his head round the door, she was likely to start throwing things.

"After lunch," Nick said blandly. "We can't intrude on them right now—Mona's fixing something special for our lunch."

"Oh, super!" one of them said, the others made enthusiastic noises. "I'd hate to have to eat the product."

I backed out of the room hastily and made for the kitchen. If Mona was expecting to feed them it was news to me. She was practically on strike, doing the absolute minimum at the slowest pace possible. The only time she had shown any animation was first thing this morning when she had come down to the kitchen carrying her handbag and placed it conspicuously on the table in the far corner. She had then insisted that the girls do the same. ("We want to be able to keep an eye on them. We don't know what sort of riff-raff we'll have tramping through the place today!") The handbags huddled on the table and Mona ostentatiously moved to block them from view whenever any of the crew walked past the doorway. It did not augur well for future relationships.

Nevertheless, Nick had plainly announced to everyone that we were going to provide lunch and it would be fatal not to, whereas to do so would be good public relations for the private restaurant service we hoped to inaugurate in the dining-room after the filming had finished.

"Does this look all right, Jean?" As I entered the

kitchen, Lexie thrust a colourful platter under my nose. Tomatoes were cut into water-lily shapes and filled with hardboiled egg yolks mixed with mayonnaise; the egg whites had been cut into star shapes, one of which perched neatly in the centre of the egg mayonnaise, the rest were scattered over the bed of lettuce leaves on which the tomatoes nestled.

"Very nice," I approved absently. Perhaps a trifle gaudy, but doubtless very photogenic. "Take them through, will you, dear?" If they weren't what was wanted, let Nick tell her. I had other problems.

Mona faced me almost as though she knew what was coming. She probably did. Nick must have mentioned it at some point if he thought she was going to do it. My dear brother had not yet assimilated just how opposed his wife was to his bright ideas.

"About lunch—" I began hesitantly.

"Yes?" There was a dangerous light in Mona's eyes.

"Er. . . Nick is expecting us to give them lunch . . . you know?"

"I know." Her tone was too pleasant, it didn't match her expression. "That's all in hand—" She gestured. "Gretel is making one of her special ragouts for them."

"You wouldn't!" I gasped. She knew how much might depend on it. "You couldn't!"

"Couldn't I?" She gave me a small deadly smile and turned away. The subject was closed.

"It's all right, Jean." Sidonie was at my elbow. "We're keeping an eye on her."

I moved cautiously towards Gretel's corner and was not reassured to find her with mortar and pestle crushing juniper berries. I had the distinct impression that the only form in which Nick's mates favoured juniper berries was distilled. They were going to wish they had stuck with the product.

I wondered if I ought to warn them. But then I carelessly allowed myself to meet Gretel's glowing eyes. Her self-confidence was restored; her pride redeemed.

Had I the right to destroy that for what might turn out to be just more of Nick's problematical pie in the sky?

"In two hours," she promised me. "Such a meal as you have never seen!"

That was what I was afraid of. Especially considering what I had already seen.

"It's all right," Sidonie murmured again; she was still at my elbow. "I'll keep a close watch."

"Fine!" I hoped I said it heartily. I smiled impartially at both of them, but put my trust in Sidonie. She had been working with us long enough to be able to spot anything potentially disastrous. Although, with Gretel, one could never be sure. She never made the same mistake twice—but she had a gift for discovering new mistakes.

I tore my gaze away from Gretel's table. She obviously considered this her big chance and was seizing it with both hands—and every condiment in the kitchen. Heady fumes arose from a large bowl in which unidentifiable cubes of meat were steeping in an alcoholic brew. (Well, she had the right idea there.)

Mona stood at the sink, her back to us, listening but unhelpful. She was hoping something would go so wrong that it would drive the interlopers out of her house for good. She did not quite dare to sabotage the proceedings herself, so she was using Gretel as her catspaw.

I moved towards the door, Sidonie moving with me. "Try to keep things under control," I said. "See that she doesn't swamp it with spices. Don't let her use too much—"

"Don't worry," Sidonie said. "She can't do much harm with that lot—and there isn't any rat poison in the house, is there?"

"If there were," I said, "Mona would have put it in Nick's coffee this morning."

From the dining-room, I heard Nick calling me. I hurried through to face whatever molehill his colleagues had blown up into a mountain, if not a smouldering volcano.

"Mashed potatoes!" Nick greeted me as though the fate

of the world depended upon instant obedience to his command. "Pyramid shape—done with the ice-cream scoop."

I froze a smile on my face as I looked around the room. The arc lights were in place, the cameras trained on a bone china place setting flanked by shimmering silver and crystal glasses. A serving dish full of the Product glittered suspiciously just modestly off-centre, not so much preserved in aspic as immobilized with varnish.

Lexie, surrounded by advertising executives, was unbuttoned to the limits of decency and laughing extravagantly at some remark that had just been made.

"Right!" I said crisply. "Mashed potatoes. Lexie, see to it! And quickly, please!"

She stopped laughing and gave me a poisonous glare. But she should have returned to the kitchen as soon as she placed her platter of tomatoes on the table. I had her dead to rights and she knew it.

Breathing deeply with indignation—a touch wasted on me—she brushed past me, ostentatiously neither speaking to me nor looking at me. From this blow, I could recover. The men watched her leave with regret.

"You've got a lot of hungry men working up an appetite here—" Nick was in the wrong for not having despatched Lexie back to the kitchen and he tried to cover it by blustering at me. "How is the lunch coming along?"

"Just fine, thank you." Revenge was sweet and instantaneous. "Gretel is taking care of it."

Nick lost colour, his jaw dropped and he closed his mouth again with a visible effort. His eyes pleaded with me to tell him I was joking. I shook my head.

"Excuse me." He gave his colleagues a sickly smile. "There's a technical detail I ought to check—"

Cravenly, I remained in the dining-room patiently moving serving dishes around the table while the camera crew decided on the most flattering angle. I kept one ear cocked towards the kitchen, but heard no major explosion. After a while, Nick returned, looking wan but not entirely desolate. Apparently some sort of compromise had been reached.

Sidonie had done an excellent job of curbing Gretel's contemplated excesses—perhaps she had tactfully taken over the cooking itself in the final stages. The meal was quite tasty, if something short of gourmet standard.

However, Nick had taken the precaution of lavishing pre-luncheon cocktails upon his friends, as well as providing several bottles of good wine with the meal. By the time they arrived at the coffee and brandy, they were decidedly mellow and just short of falling off their chairs. Which was exactly the way Nick wanted them. If any of them felt unwell later in the afternoon, they would attribute it to overindulgence in the alcoholic refreshment rather than suspect the meal itself.

By the time we had cleared the dishes away and they had reeled back to the business end of the table, we had three bookings for private parties and a preliminary enquiry about catering for the agency's next Christmas party.

So far, so good.

Nick was bustling about trying to look more sober than the others and be helpful while they went on shooting. I realized that he was trying to keep their minds off the promised tour of the kitchen until the girls had had a chance to finish the washing up and the place did not look quite so sordid.

The afternoon's shooting proceeded at a slower pace than the morning's since the technicians were no longer so sure whether it was the cameras or their eyes which were out of focus. It couldn't move slowly enough to suit me; I hoped that they would reach the hour at which some fervid union member would call "time" and they would all depart so swiftly that Nick would have no chance to further his Machiavellian schemes.

It was a vain hope, of course. Nick had never in all his

life let his eyes waver from the main chance and he was keeping watch on the clock, too.

"Tea-time!" He struck just as the clock struck four. "Suppose we pop into the kitchen and see if we can organize a cup of tea?"

I had been waiting for something like that. I backed out of the doorway as Nick and his executive chums started forward. I was in the kitchen well before they could get there, ready to try one last gambit to keep the peace.

"Mona," I said, "I'm sorry, but I'm terribly tied up with this lot. Do you think you could nip up to my flat and get me my—?"

"I will go!" Gretel was still aglow with her triumph. I shook my head at her, but she was beyond signals. "Was it not wonderful?" She started for the door. "Every scrap off their plates, they eat!" She did not have triumphs like that often. "Nothing was left! They truly enjoyed it!"

On a wave of euphoria, she sailed through the doorway and up the stairs without having noticed that I had not told her what I wanted fetched. Mona remained by the stove, watching me suspiciously. Lexie and Sidonie paused by the cupboard where they were stacking the dishes away, looking at both of us warily, as though conscious of a gathering storm.

"Mona, dear—" I began again, but too late.

"Hello, my loves." Nick stood in the doorway, the various directors massed behind him. "What about a spot of tea for some parched throats?" He led the others into the kitchen.

"We're busy," Mona said abruptly. "We can't have people underfoot."

"We'll make it ourselves." He smiled ingratiatingly. "You girls gave us a magnificent meal, we ought to be able to make a pot of tea for ourselves. Just carry on with what you were doing—don't let us disturb you."

Stepping forward, he put an arm around Mona's shoulders and moved her to one side. "We can manage," he said reassuringly. "You just take it easy."

Behind him, one of the directors gasped. "Look at that!"

The Aga was in plain view now, a cauldron bubbling at the back, a kettle humming on a front hob. On the wall behind it, a range of copper-bottomed utensils shone in the artificial light. Bags of dried herbs, suspended from the ceiling, swayed gently from the motion of bodies moving past. Strings of onions, garlic, red and green peppers, sausages . . .

Even I had to admit that the effect was supremely photogenic, although I noted that most of the more picturesque items had been moved into the kitchen from the larder at some time when I hadn't been paying attention and, obviously, neither had Mona.

"What a scene!" the man (was he the Artistic Director?) said. "What a fantastic setting!"

"Is it?" Nick blinked with surprise. As though viewing the kitchen for the first time through different eyes, he stepped back, raised his hands in front of his eyes, making a frame of them, and peered through it intently.

"Yes," he acknowledged slowly, as though bowing to superior wisdom. "Yes, I suppose it is."

"No!" Mona hurled herself forward to stand in front of the Aga, arms spread out defensively, as though protecting it from vandals. "Oh no you don't!"

"Your soup is boiling over, dear," Nick warned mildly.

"Oh no!" Mona whirled and dashed to bend over the steaming cauldron. It was nowhere near boiling over, of course, but she gave it a precautionary stir and then automatically lifted the sipping spoon to her lips to taste it, presenting them with just the picture Nick had been angling for.

"Bloody marvellous!" one of them said. "Nick, you crafty old sod, how long have you been keeping this one up your sleeve?"

"She *is* good, isn't she?" Nick said modestly. "Just looking at her, you *know* that soup is going to be perfection itself."

"Bloody marvellous!" the man said again, pivoting slowly to take in all the aspects of the kitchen. He raised his voice. "Bert! Come through here a minute, will you? Bring a camera!"

"No!" Mona stepped forward, facing Nick as though she might spring at him like a tigress. "Not *my* house! Not *my* kitchen?" All that saved him was that she hadn't realized yet that he was planning to use her, as well.

"It's my house, too," Nick reminded her unforgivably. "And my kitchen."

"Oh!" That did it. She struck so swiftly Nick had no time to dodge. The wooden spoon she was still holding broke with the force of the blow and Nick went reeling.

Mona ran from the room, grabbing blindly for her handbag from the table and pushing past the men clustered around Nick. We heard the front door slam behind her.

"Poor girl." Nick smiled weakly, nursing his jaw. "She's overwhelmed, that's all."

The men nodded, accepting the explanation. In their world, people queued up—on their knees, if necessary—for the opportunity to become a public figure through television exposure. They could not imagine that anyone might find it repugnant.

Nick didn't deserve sympathy. I let the men struggle to lift him into the rocking-chair and crossed the kitchen to join Sidonie and Lexie. Sidonie was holding a handbag in her hands—it was Mona's.

"She went off with mine," Sidonie said. "She couldn't see what she was doing, she was crying so."

"She'll be back as soon as she's calmed down a bit," I heard Nick assuring his colleagues. I looked across the room at him.

"Don't bet on it," I said.

Chapter
15

We decided to let Nick stew in his own juice for a while.

Sidonie had called me on my private line much later that night. "It's all right, Jean. Mona's here."

"Thank heavens!" Of course, I had been fairly certain that Mona wouldn't do anything desperate—she wasn't the suicidal type—but it was a relief to know where she was and that she was safe.

"I'm afraid she doesn't want to speak to you," Sidonie said hesitantly. "In fact, she doesn't know I'm calling, but I thought I ought to."

"Quite right," I said. "But it might be better not to let her know that you've contacted me until she's—er—less upset. She *is* still upset, I suppose?" It was an unnecessary question; if Mona wasn't still upset, she'd have come home.

"I'm afraid so," Sidonie said. "Oh, not with you, especially, but with Nick . . . and the way things have been going."

"I know," I said.

"It was quite sensible of her to come here," Sidonie said. "Of course, as soon as she realized she had my handbag, she wanted to return it. And it had my keys in it, so we found her waiting for us when we got back. I don't think she quite knew where else to go."

"I suppose she didn't." Most of Mona's old friends—the ones she hadn't shared with Nick and who could be trusted not to give her away—lived up near the Scottish border. It was one thing to take Sidonie's handbag in honest mistake for her own, but it would have been beyond Mona's sense of propriety to use money from it.

"She can stay here with us for a few days while she cools down," Sidonie said. "There's plenty of room. And we'll be able to smuggle whatever she needs to her."

"That's a good idea," I approved. It was certainly a lot better than having Mona wander off again and disappear to heaven knows where. "Do you think she'll agree?"

"I think so," Sidonie said. "So long as we promise not to let Nick know where she is."

"That's fine with me," I said. "Let him squirm a bit. He has it coming!"

For the remainder of the week, Nick went not-so-quietly to pieces. In front of his advertising chums, who were still cluttering up the dining-room, he maintained the pretence that Mona had been called away to care for her sick mother. At the end of the day, when they had all gone, he paced the kitchen, raging.

"Where *is* she? Where can she have gone? I've rung everyone we ever knew and none of them have seen her. She can't just have vanished off the face of the earth!"

"People do." Lexie twisted the knife with concealed glee. "You hear about it all the time. They're never found again. That's because most people disappear to escape from an intolerable situation. The police know that, that's why they don't break their necks to find anyone unless it's someone under age, or they think there was something suspicious about the disappearance." She smiled sweetly at Nick. "*Have* you gone to the police, yet?"

"No!" She knew he had not. He was terrified of the

possible publicity, of all his friends finding out that his wife had left him. Unless or until Mona was found floating in the Thames, Nick would keep the police out of it.

"Oooh," Gretel mourned. "It is so sad, so terrible. This was always such a happy place and now... now..." She broke off, choking back sobs. We had decided that it was safer not to tell her that Mona was all right. In the kindness of her heart, she might have blurted it out to Nick and put him out of his misery. As it was, Gretel's air of being in a house of bereavement was undermining Nick's nerves far more effectively than any sniping we could do.

"You should not stand here and do nothing." Gretel appealed to Nick with desperate earnestness. "You should call for Scotland Yard—if it is not already too late!"

"Oh no!" Sidonie said quickly, as Nick looked irresolute. "It's much too early to think about the police. I'm sure Mona will come back as soon as she'd had a bit of time to cool down."

"Perhaps she's got amnesia." Wickedly, Lexie stirred it up a bit more. "The way she rushed out of here, she might have tripped and fallen and hit her head. She could be wandering around somewhere, not knowing who she is or where she belongs—"

"Oh, that is terrible!" Gretel gasped. "It cannot be allowed. You *must* go to Scotland Yard!"

"We have no reason to believe anything of the sort has happened." I divided an icy look between Gretel and Lexie. "I suggest we keep calm."

"That's all very well for you to say." Nick was perspiring visibly. "You aren't lying awake most of the night thinking about all the terrible things that might have happened to her. And when I do sleep," he brooded, "I have nightmares."

"Oh, poor man!" Gretel said. If she had known the truth, she would have blurted it out at that moment. The rest of us were made of sterner stuff.

"You've always been subject to nightmares," I reminded him. I could remember many childhood nights disturbed by

Nick's sudden shouts of rage or alarm. "You've even had nightmares when an advertising campaign was going badly."

"Little sister—" he glared at me bitterly—"you were ever such a comfort to me."

"You brought this on yourself," I said. "You know Mona never wanted any part of turning her home into a three-ring circus."

"It's my home, too," he muttered sulkily.

"*And* you've pointed that out once too often. You should have known better."

"I'm *sure* everything is going to be all right." Sidonie intervened hastily, unwilling to be witness to what was devolving into a sibling squabble. Lexie snorted with suppressed laughter; a family fight was her idea of light entertainment. "Mona is bound to come back soon."

"She'd better hurry. Perhaps you've forgotten—" Nick had a try at spreading the alarm and despondency. "Your Charity Ball is next week and we're short-handed as it is. If Mona doesn't come back, you're going to have to pay for extra help, she does as much work as two or three people."

"I'm *certain* she won't let us down." Sidonie was in danger of giving the game away by being too unworried. She seemed to realize this just in time. "And anyway," she added, "Lexie and I can slip behind the scenes and help out, if necessary. No one will mind if we do."

"*I'll* mind!" Lexie protested. "You may enjoy playing High Priestess of the Pantry, but I'm looking forward to being one of the guests for a change. It isn't fair if you're going to make me work. It's my evening off!"

"You needn't worry." Sidonie gave her cousin a cold look. "I'm *sure* Mona won't let us down."

Spring flowered abruptly that week. It might not last but, for the evening of the charity ball, it was present in all its glory. The marquee crouched in a field of daffodils rippled by the mildest and warmest of breezes. Rush torches flamed on both sides of the curving carriageway.

"But how funny!" Gretel exclaimed. "I did not expect a tent—even such a big one. Why do they not have the ball indoors?"

"It's a charity ball," Nick said. "Not a private party."

"And so?" Gretel was unenlightened.

"The trouble with a charity ball," I explained, "is that anyone can buy a ticket and come. There's no control over the guest list. People who have houses big enough to hold a ball in don't like the idea of a lot of strangers roaming through their house and noticing what valuables they have and where they're kept. There's too much danger of an uninvited return visit some night."

"People would do this?" Gretel sounded aghast.

"They do it all the time," Nick assured her. "Burglars even read the glossy magazines devoted to beautiful homes. That's why so many of the photographs are so lifeless. The collections of snuff-boxes, the antique silver service, the Old Masters, have been removed from view before the photographer is allowed to start work. These days people have to be very careful about giving the impression that they have anything worth stealing."

Inside the marquee, the polished wooden floor was beginning to sound less hollow and strange as more people crowded in. Long wooden tables ran the length of the far side, set with clusters of champagne-filled glasses at intervals. The hum of talk and laughter grew; the band tuned up their instruments.

"The weather could not be more perfect!" Gretel babbled. "Oh, Sidonie, you are so lucky!"

"Yee-es," Sidonie said dubiously, her gaze roving up and down the table and across the tent. I knew the feeling. Sidonie was not going to enthuse—or even relax—until the evening was safely over. "So far, so good," was as much as she would admit at the moment.

Later in the evening, we would take over the long trestle tables and set out dainty sandwiches and the obligatory strawberries and cream. I had spent the morning carefully hulling the fiendishly expensive hothouse strawberries and had not been pleased to find that—even at the price we paid—some of them were already turning soft and squishy. It was as well we were using them tonight.

So far as I was concerned, I would be happy to see strawberries lose their reputation as a luxury food. It was not generally known that strawberries contain a toxic agent, cocemarin, which holds back the clotting of blood. People recovering from coronary thrombosis are often treated with the chemical. If they were to eat strawberries, or any food to which cocemarin had been added, haemorrhage could result. It as an obscure worry, perhaps, but in these days when doctors did not always think to warn their patients of the side-effects of new drugs—if, indeed, they were aware of them themselves—it behooved caterers to be aware of the more obscure dangers of otherwise innocent foods. Almost anything could be deadly—if the wrong person ate it. But how did you know who the wrong person was? You couldn't stand at the door handing out questionnaires about allergies.

I returned my attention to the present situation. Later still this evening—or, rather, tomorrow morning—we would serve breakfast to the dawn patrol. Chafing dishes were primed and waiting in the van. Sidonie's early birthday present, a large microwave oven, already occupied pride of place at the far end of the table and several of her friends had been admiring it. Strong hints were obviously going to be dropped to other fathers as gift-giving times approached.

"And oh! you look so beautiful, Sidonie," Gretel said.

It was true. Sidonie was radiant in a shimmering gold and aquamarine gown that brought out unsuspected green highlights in her eyes. For once, she was the centre of most of the attention and beginning to allow herself to enjoy it. Lexie, in a demure, improbably virginal white gown, seemed to be in a self-effacing mode—which was most unlike her. Perhaps she felt that this was so much Sidonie's night that there was no point in trying to compete. Although her colour was high and there was a glint of devilment in her eyes to signal that, at any moment, her mood might change.

There was little hope of that with Mona. Although she had arrived shortly after the rest of us and donned her uniform, she was making it very clear that she was neither forgiving nor forgetting. She was keeping as much space as possible between herself and Nick, ignoring smiles, waves, and anything that might be classed as an overture.

It was going to be a long hard night. Sidonie and Lexie moved away to mingle with the guests and I realized just how much I was going to miss their familiar moral support.

Gretel was humming under her breath and moving restlessly in rhythm with the music; the dancing had now started. I sent her out to help Nick carry in things from the van. That would work off some of her energy.

I moved towards Mona, who had stationed herself as far away from the rest of us as possible, but she gave me a cold blank look and turned away. Obviously, I was too much my brother's sister to be welcome company. I hoped she would thaw out as the night wore on. We were going to have to work together as a close team when the serving started.

Right now, it was the turn of the wine waiters. They were circling the tables armed with champagne bottles, topping up glasses. As I looked around the tent, I began to pick out familiar faces.

Roddy had just led Lexie out on to the dance floor, watched sullenly by Humpty, who was sitting at a nearby table with a couple of Hooray Henrys who were holding out their glasses as the wine waiter approached, obviously determined to get as much as possible of everything going. At these prices, one could scarcely call them freeloaders and I suspected a large part of Humpty's sullenness was due to the fact that this was one party he had had to pay for instead of crash. Sidonie would have seen to that.

Tristram Quardon and Edda Price were prowling the periphery of the tent looking for their table. Both appeared rather strained and weary. I wondered if there were more trouble brewing back at Quardon International.

I became aware of Ongar Manganian, followed by his Italian shadow, walking towards me. He was frowning as he surveyed the array of glasses ranged on the pristine white tablecloth, unmarred by any suggestion of food in the offing.

"You are here," he greeted me. "So presumably we will eat at some time."

"Not for a while yet," Aldo said with a lazy grin. "You're supposed to dance first, you know."

"In all the time I have known you—" Ongar glowered at his aide—"this is the first time I have detected a taint of madness. Are you truly insane—or do you think I am? In any event," he added, "there is no one here I wish to dance with. Not on the right side of the table. Is that not true?"

"Quite true." Aldo gave me a look which was obviously intended to be flattering. I began to edge away. Sidonie might not mind, but other people might take a dim view of the help fraternizing with the guests, much less monopolizing the lion of the evening. And Ongar Manganian was very much the lion of any occasion he chose to honour. Already there were several pretty little vultures circling their intended prey.

"*There* you are, Ongar—" While the younger ones were still circling, a more experienced one swooped. "Now come along. It's time you took your place on the dance floor."

"Don't worry." She gave me a bright unseeing look and a blank dismissive smile which put me in my place. "I'll bring him back when you start serving the food."

She wouldn't be able to keep him away when we began serving the food—and she knew it.

"Lady Pamela," I explained to Nick, who had just come up behind me. "Lexie's mother."

"Like mother, like daughter," he shrugged. "That's a nice dress she's almost wearing."

It was fair comment and also, possibly, the reason Lexie was dressed with such unusual demureness. Not because of any deference to Sidonie's position tonight, but because she didn't want to compete with her own mother. Word had it that Lady Pamela was a Tartar when crossed.

Of course, Lexie was rather like that, too. I caught a glimpse of her face over Roddy's shoulder as she watched her mother coax Ongar Manganian on to the dance floor. For a split second, just before Roddy murmured something to her and she turned back to him, her face was murderous with rage.

Did she really imagine she had a chance of snaring Ongar? Or that her mother did? I felt certain the wily magnate was more than a match for both of them—although not in the way they hoped. He had escaped ladies of higher rank and greater fortune in his time.

Although, to be honest, he had also succumbed with enough frequency and unexpectedness to allow any woman, of whatever station, to hope. And he was reputed to be generous—very generous—when the fancy took him. Perhaps Lexie and Lady Pamela were not so far out in their ambitions, after all.

Tristram Quardon and Edda Price had also been watching the by-play. I wondered how Tristram would like it if his sister-in-law were to become the wife—or mistress—of his latest associate. Edda looked worried, but Tristram's face was expressionless. He would probably prefer to see Lady Pamela in that position than Lexie.

Despite the currents swirling beneath the surface, the evening went well until we served the strawberries and cream while the band were taking their midnight break. Then the trouble started.

The champagne had been flowing a little too freely. There were always a few who would take advantage. It was not inevitable that something should happen, but the odds were heavily in favour of it.

I was aware of a growing disturbance, which seemed to centre around Humpty's table and to be spreading outwards from there. I couldn't see what was happening, though, and remained puzzled until a strawberry suddenly struck my cheek splattering cream over my uniform.

I dabbed at the cream with a napkin and looked around. Suddenly the air was full of flying strawberries trailing droplets of cream like the tails of comets. There were shrieks and scuffles as those caught in the crossfire tried to get out of the way.

"Oh, really!" Edda Price had just taken a dish of strawberries and cream from the table in front of me. "This is disgraceful! So—so juvenile!"

What did she expect? It was the younger ones doing it. I heard Lexie's shrill giggle just a split-second before a squishy strawberry exploded against Edda's elaborate coiffure, dripping red juice and cream down her face and on to her black velvet gown. It seemed as though a few grudges were being worked off tonight. My own strawberry had told me that Humpty had not really forgiven me for throwing him out the time he had gate-crashed.

"Here—" I handed Edda the napkin I had been using.

"It's no use—" She tidied herself as best she could. "This will have to go to the cleaners. Oh, why are people so thoughtless?"

"It's a form of upper-class insolence." Tristram Quardon had joined us. "If you can't afford to have your clothes ruined at one of these affairs, then you can't afford to attend at all and shouldn't be here. I've seen it before, but not in a good many years." His lips tightened. "The Bright Young Sods at play! There was a lot of it at one time, but it died out when life got tougher. I'm sorry to see it coming back again. I'm sorrier still to see Lexie out there with them."

With them? She was one of the ringleaders. Crimson-splattered, she and Humpty appeared to be leading one group against another, none of whom were familiar to me.

The floor had been cleared of all except the combatants now. Several of the older people were shouting vainly for order.

"Oh, they are not nice!" Gretel wailed. "They should

not behave so at such a lovely party. Look at poor Sidonie—they are ruining her evening.''

Pale with fury, Sidonie was skirting the edge of the battle, waving frantically at Lexie and Humpty, trying to restore some sort of order. She was having no more success than her elders. She seemed to realize that it was going to take more than her efforts and slipped out of the tent for reinforcements.

As I watched, a girl dashed up to the table, exchanged an empty dish for one full of strawberries and dashed back into the fray.

''Right!'' Nick said grimly. I had not noticed him come up behind me. ''That does it. Let's withdraw the ammunition. That will put a stop to it.''

We swiftly began to remove the strawberries from view, working together as a team again. Mona was handing dishes to Nick without seeming to notice it. Our one concern was to clear the table before anyone else could come and collect more ammunition. When they had used the last of their own strawberries, the battle would be over.

Out of the corner of my eye, I saw Sidonie leading the band back into the tent. They took in the situation and went quickly to the bandstand, taking up their instruments.

As quickly as it had begun, the battle was petering out. As the band began to play again, a few brave couples got up to dance, keeping well to the edge of the floor.

''I'm sorry about this,'' Tristram Quardon said to us. ''I'll speak to Lexie about it.''

But Lexie had noticed our heads turning in her direction and was bright enough to guess the gist of the remarks being made. One moment she was there, the next moment she had disappeared. Probably gone to clean up—and hide out—in the rest room until she thought the coast was clear again.

If she was smart, she'd stay there a long time.

Chapter
16

"Fools!" Ongar Manganian was shaking with rage. "Wicked, stupid fools!"

"Should they be dancing so soon?" Gretel worried. "The floor is slippery. Someone may fall and be hurt."

"Serve them bloody well right," Nick said, still grim. "Except that it's always the wrong ones who get hurt." Lexie was still missing.

"It's all right." Sidonie was still upset, but trying to smile for the benefit of any onlookers. "We're insured for that. For all sorts of contingencies. And people will be careful. As soon as this set ends, we'll have the floor cleaned and then it will be perfectly safe."

"Wicked!" Ongar raged again. "It should never have happened. Such wickedness! Such stupidity! Such fools!"

"Oh, nonsense!" Lady Pamela said lightly. "They're just high-spirited. We were always larking about like that when I was a deb. You're making far too much of it. You were young once yourself, weren't you?"

"Young, yes. Stupid, never!" The look he turned on her must have told her that she had just blasted any chance she might have had with him, even before he continued speaking.

"When I was young," he said softly, bitterly, "when I was a little boy, we never play with food. There was famine in Armenia. You know what that means?"

"I'm sorry." Lady Pamela stepped back involuntarily, as though physically shoved by the intensity of his rage and contempt.

"It means no food. No play, even. It means crawling in the gutter, picking up and eating the grape pips the rich have spat out. Eating them, maybe with the dirt and spittle still on them—yes, and fighting other scavenging children for the privilege—because we were starving. Because there is a little nourishment in them that will help us to survive maybe one more day."

Lady Pamela shuddered and stepped farther back.

"But here—here they make games with food. Throw it at each other. Splash champagne like sea-water. And laugh. Laugh! They do not know—"

"I'll speak severely to Lexie—" But Lady Pamela might as well have not spoken.

"They laugh at me. I know it. They call me 'The Starving Armenian' because I like to eat. But they do not know how right they are. I starved once, yes. But never again. I make a vow when I am a little boy. I will grow up and never again will I be hungry. I make millions—billions—and I tell you, if necessary, I spend every penny of it on food—

"*You!*" He whirled on me. "*You* understand what I mean!"

"Yes." I shrank back before the burning intensity of his gaze, but he was right. I did know what he meant. Working in catering, surrounded by food, experimenting with it, trying new ways to prepare it and present it, the essential nature of it was rarely considered.

With food, you lived; without food, you died. It was as basic as that.

You could chop it, mince it, spice it, colour it, shape it into unlikely forms, try to disguise it any way you please. You could fry it, boil it, bake it, grill it, sauté it, flambé it—as though all your preoccupation with the process could mask the real reason for it.

Diet faddists carried on as though there were no need for people to indulge themselves in it at all. Psychologists further obscured the issue with various theories that food was love, or an anodyne for boredom. But the truth remained.

"Food is life." Ongar Manganian nodded at me. "In this country, you have not learned this the hard way. To treat food with disrespect is to mock at life itself. You should not be surprised that there are many peoples who despise you for it. And if, some day, the tumbrils roll, you will have only yourselves to blame!"

If Lexie could have heard that conversation, she wouldn't have returned to the ball at all. As it was, she remained in her retreat for at least half an hour before she ventured into the marquee again.

I spotted her deep in conversation with Humpty in a shadowed corner. Both of them were suspiciously animated and unsubdued by the disapproval they had generated earlier.

Her mother and Tristram Quardon spotted them just then. From different points, they moved to converge on Lexie, but some sixth sense warned her in time.

Once again Lexie did her disappearing act, leaving behind, not a puff of smoke, but a blinking bewildered Humpty, looking around for the companion he had been talking to just a split second before. Then he realized that the enemy was still advancing, determined to create an unpleasant scene with him in lieu of Lexie.

He wasn't as fast as she was, but he was just as determined. He lumbered away, putting several dancing couples between himself and the Quardons before he found a loose flap in the tent and slipped through it to safety.

Lady Pamela and Tristram Quardon suddenly became

aware that they were heading for a direct confrontation with each other, with the reason for it no longer in sight. They locked hostile implacable glances for a moment, then averted their eyes and returned to their respective tables.

It was some time before I saw either Lexie or Humpty again. Not until we were starting the preparations for breakfast. By then, the crowd had thinned considerably. Most of the older generation had left, as had the younger ones who had to think about getting up and reporting to work later that morning. Only the diehards were left.

We had decided to cook the sausages on the spot in the microwave oven, browning them in a chafing dish before serving. We had Gretel working at the microwave oven since the sight of sausages emerging seemingly as raw as when they had entered would be less unnerving to her than to the rest of us. She was accustomed to mishaps like that and, once we had assured her that the sausages were truly cooked, despite appearances, she accepted our word happily. Cooking was largely an act of faith with her at the best of times.

I set containers of cold scrambled eggs and another container of toast behind Gretel in readiness. For those who wanted it, she could heap the cold scrambled egg on the cold toast and then pop it into the microwave to heat in seconds. We were fairly certain she could handle that safely.

Just in case, Mona was stationed next to her, between the chafing dishes of browning sausages and devilled kidneys. She could quickly lend a hand if problems developed.

I would take care of the kedgeree and creamed mushrooms, while Nick manned the coffee urn beyond me. Mona had gone back to keeping him as distant as was possible. We had set out a tray of Danish pastries on the other side of the coffee urn in the hope of keeping the queue moving so that they wouldn't congregate around the coffee urn and create an obstruction.

It was ironic, in the light of what had happened earlier,

that we had vetoed serving bread rolls on the grounds that they were the traditional weapons when a youthful gathering got rowdy and began throwing things.

At a nearby table, Ongar Manganian was watching our preparations intently. So was Aldo, but without the intentness, and giving us an occasional approving nod. I wondered if his family catered for many outside functions or whether they confined all their efforts to the restaurant. Perhaps someday I would lunch at that restaurant and have a quiet look round—if I could find it, if one word of the story he had told me was true.

Roddy Bletchley had drawn Tristram Quardon aside for what looked like one of those corridor conferences. Unfortunately, there was no corridor available and Roddy was obviously feeling the lack. He glanced around unhappily and settled for guiding Tristram over to the corner where Gretel was working. He frowned at Gretel, but she was too intent on her relays of sausages to notice. This seemed to reassure Roddy—or perhaps he remembered that Gretel wasn't English and decided that the nuances of an involved business conversation conducted in lowered tones would escape her. He began talking earnestly to Tristram Quardon.

From her table, Edda Price watched them as though wishing she could lip-read.

That was when I saw Lexie and Humpty re-enter the marquee. They split up almost as soon as they were inside and moved off in different directions. Lexie was still obviously trying to avoid an encounter with either her mother or her uncle, but she seemed to have recovered some of her assurance. She joined a group of friends and, very shortly, her laugh was ringing out.

Meanwhile, Humpty was circling the marquee moving ever closer to the buffet table, as though stalking game. His eyes were every bit as greedily intense as those of Ongar Manganian, but he had not the excuse of childhood starvation.

"Are you ready?" Sidonie came up, glancing at her

watch. "If we start soon, we might have a chance of clearing this lot before dawn." She stifled a yawn. "I'm beginning to feel that I've had enough of them all."

"Ready any time you are," I agreed. Those watching must have seen my head nod. There was a sudden stampede.

Humpty beat Ongar Manganian by a short head, snatching the first serving of scrambled eggs from Gretel. He then preceded Ongar the length of the table, heaping his plate, taking more than his share from every serving dish.

Fuming, Ongar followed Humpty, but not taking quite so much. "I will come back," he promised. Behind him, Aldo carefully duplicated—in smaller portions—everything his master had chosen.

The others crowded along then and we were so busy that I had no time to notice anything more until the first rush was over.

"Kedgeree, please." The voice was familiar and I looked up to find Roddy holding out two plates. "I thought I'd get them both something to eat," he explained, gesturing. "It might help to ease the situation."

I followed the direction of his gesture and saw that Tristram Quardon had cornered Lexie at last. Neither of them looked happy about it, in direct contrast to Gretel, who was ecstatic at having such a promising conversation within earshot. I hoped she wouldn't drop any dishes while trying not to miss a word.

"Tris is pretty upset," Roddy confided. "Not that I blame him. Lexie is a bit much sometimes."

As he spoke, Tristram Quardon shook his head in exasperation and seemed about to abandon his niece, perhaps for all time. Lexie stretched out an imploring hand and caught his sleeve. She began talking rapidly, earnestly, head dipped like a penitent. Tristram's face remained stern but the atmosphere between them seemed to be lightening.

Roddy hurried back to them with the kedgeree and they accepted the plates gratefully, taking the opportunity to declare a tacit truce. Roddy returned for a plate for himself, looking as though he had just accomplished a good day's work.

I was beginning to feel that way myself. Everyone had been fed and we had plenty in reserve for second helpings. They were all seated at tables and the hum of contented conversation was rising.

Sidonie spoke to the band and they rose and came over to the buffet. We had another brief flurry of activity. When it was over, I approached Nick at the coffee urn.

"I think we all deserve a cup of coffee," I said.

"Before the second wave hits us," he agreed. "Our Starving Armenian looks just about ready for more." He filled a cup and handed it to me. "Anyway, they seem to be enjoying—"

At that moment, Humpty lurched to his feet, gave a cry of agony and, clutching his stomach, pitched to the floor.

All conversation stopped abruptly.

"I'm dying!" Humpty howled, rolling about on the floor. "I've been poisoned."

Ongar Manganian stopped eating abruptly and pushed his plate away. It was an historic sight to witness, but I would have given anything not to have seen it. Not when Executive Meal Service had been doing the cooking.

"Dying . . ." Humpty had a penetrating whine. "Poisoned . . ."

Aldo gave me an encouraging nod and determinedly— ostentatiously—continued eating.

No one else was prepared to be so sporting. The band members hurriedly deposited their plates at their feet and took up their instruments, looking around uncertainly, waiting for some signal from someone.

"I hope they're not thinking of playing 'Nearer, my God, to Thee,' " Nick muttered between clenched teeth. "That would be all we needed."

"Those sausages!" Mona was beside us, all differences

forgotten, joining forces against a common danger. "Nick, has the deep-freeze been working all right?"

"The deep-freeze is all right!" Nick snarled. "This has nothing to do with us. He brought it on himself. Did you see the way he loaded his plate? That fellow eats like a hog at swilling time!"

"Of course," I said with relief. "That must be it." Humpty's overburdened stomach had rebelled at last, presenting him with a richly deserved bout of indigestion. It was simply unfortunate that it had had to happen here.

I turned just in time to see Tristram Quardon sway and fall.

Nick vaulted the table, then hesitated. But Tristram Quardon lay quietly, while Humpty was howling his head off. Nick took a deep breath and advanced on Humpty.

I dashed up to the end of the table, ducked underneath, and knelt beside Tristram Quardon.

"I did not do anything," Gretel whimpered, cowering behind the microwave oven. "It is not my fault."

"Shut up, Gretel," I said absently. "No one is blaming you." He lay there, preternaturally still, and I had to steel myself to reach for his wrist and try to find his pulse.

Mona, with her customary presence of mind, had dashed off to telephone for an ambulance. Sidonie, wringing her hands, had gone first to Humpty, and was now hovering over me. Lexie was pressed back against the table as though trying to dissociate herself from everything.

"Is he all right?" Sidonie wailed. "First Humpty, now Tristram? What's happening?"

"Nothing." I fought a grim, defensive battle. "They've just been taken ill suddenly, that's all. It's been a long night—and Tristram wasn't in the best of health to begin with."

"No! No, you must not deceive yourself." Ongar Manganian had hurried to his fallen colleague's side, but his eyes still watched Humpty. "It was intended for me, the poison. He pushed ahead of me . . . took my place . . . took the food intended for me . . .''

"Don't be absurd!" I pulled myself upright, forgetting Tristram Quardon momentarily. "There was nothing wrong with the food!"

"Oh, Jean—" Lexie, in her turn, was swaying. "Jean—I hate to tell you this—" Abruptly she sank to the floor, knees drawn up in a foetal position.

"Jean—I'm afraid I'm not feeling very well myself."

Chapter
17

The waiting-room of the nearby hospital was overflowing by the time we had all crowded into it. It was as well they had no other emergencies on hand. We must have looked like ghosts from the proverbial feast as we paced the floor awaiting news of our fallen ones, who were upstairs having their stomachs pumped.

Ongar Manganian stroked his stomach thoughtfully, his eyes darting from side to side as though some unseen enemy might suddenly launch an attack.

Aldo had taken advantage of the situation to put an arm round me. In just a few more minutes I was going to pull away and give him an icy look, but not quite yet. I rested my head against his shoulder, trying to think.

It must have been the fish . . . it *had* to be the fish.

Humpty had eaten generous portions of everything, but Lexie and Tristram had eaten only the kedgeree. But Roddy had eaten it, too, and he seemed to be all right. And what about all the others? Surely, if the fish were tainted, many more guests from the ball would be upstairs having their stomachs pumped.

Perhaps the fish was like the curate's egg, only parts of it were bad . . .

"I don't see how it could have happened," Sidonie said. "We were always so careful."

"Please, my friends, you must not blame yourselves." Ongar Manganian tried to comfort us. "I have enemies. This could have happened anywhere, at any time. I have always known that."

"Do you mean—" Nick spoke with dangerous quietness— "because *you* have enemies, *our* reputations have been blasted into oblivion?"

Ongar shrugged. "It is entirely possible," he admitted.

"By God," Nick said, "if I thought that, I'd murder you myself!"

Aldo stirred uneasily and I found myself restraining him. "No, no," I murmured. "Nick doesn't mean it. He just talks for effect."

Ongar Manganian seemed to realize this. "I will make it up to you," he promised, unworried.

"Make it up to us? How can you?" Nick choked with fury. "You have no idea what we stand to lose. The business we've built up, the plans for the future. If this gets into the newspapers, we won't even be used for photographic sessions!"

Sudden hope flared in Mona's eyes. One person's hell was someone else's heaven. But why did they always have to marry each other?

"We don't know yet—" Aldo spoke cautiously—"that the food was responsible."

"We will before long." I refused to admit false hope. "They took away samples of everything. We ought to have the laboratory reports in a day or so."

"Sooner than that!" Ongar Manganian was indignant. "You do not imagine I would leave something of such importance to your public health authorities? I have made my own arrangements with a private laboratory! Even now, they are conducting their tests. The instant they have finished, I will have the results. Then we may know with whom we are dealing. And—'' his expression was grim—''I will take steps!''

''We should also get a report from the hospital authorities here,'' Aldo reminded him. ''As soon as they've analysed the stomach contents.''

''My poor, poor little girl.'' Lady Pamela gave a long, shuddering sigh. Roddy Bletchley, who had been hovering like a dragonfly between Lady Pamela and Edda Price, darted to comfort her.

''It is unfortunate.'' Ongar gave her a cold look. ''But your daughter is receiving the best of care. They all are.'''

That much was true. Motivated as much by guilt as by genuine concern, Ongar Manganian had ordered private rooms for the victims, disturbed the slumber of his Harley Street specialist and had him rushed to the hospital to take charge personally, and it appeared that he had a toxicologist and laboratory on tap. It was one way of making sure he was kept informed and with a minimum of red tape.

Perhaps we should be grateful, but I found that I could not believe in some mysterious enemy who had set out to poison Ongar Manganian and struck down innocent people instead. I wished I could believe it. It was a more comforting theory than the possibility that some negligence in our kitchen was responsible for the outbreak. If that were to be proved, how sympathetic would Ongar Manganian be then?

I shuddered. If only Mona had been supervising the kitchen for the past week, I would feel on surer ground. But Nick and Gretel had been holding the fort while I was in and out attending to the business luncheons with Lexie and Sidonie. There was no way of telling what might have happened behind my back.

Nick, preoccupied with his own concerns, might not have noticed the deep-freeze acting up again until it was too late and the defrosting process had already started. It would be entirely like him then to readjust the thermostat and leave everything to re-freeze without bothering to mention it to me.

And Gretel—who knew what Gretel might have done as she blundered helpfully about the kitchen? Gretel was surely the weakest link in our chain. Anything was possible with her. *Had* she made some deadly mistake? She was acting as guilty as Typhoid Mary about to be unmasked yet again. Why were people who could have such a devastating effect on food so irresistibly drawn to it?

Gretel was sobbing in a corner now. Edda Price stood over her uneasily, her thoughts obviously elsewhere. Somewhere upstairs with Tristram Quardon, who had been the worst-hit of the trio.

And yet, that in itself was odd. He and Lexie had been almost the last to eat. What sort of micro-organism could act so quickly? Humpty had been the first to collect his food and wolf it down, it was not so surprising that he might have succumbed.

But what of all the other guests who had eaten in between the first and the last to be served? I pulled away and studied Aldo. He looked fine. So did Ongar Manganian. Yet they had been immediately behind Humpty in the serving queue.

"How do you feel?" I asked Aldo.

"Absolutely fine." He knew what I meant. "Not a quiver or a collywoble. Don't worry." He patted me reassuringly. "The food was delicious and I don't see how there could have been anything wrong with it." He frowned. "But there's something wrong with the pattern of the attacks—"

"Unless—" The first numbing shock was wearing off now and I was beginning to think more clearly. "Humpty *did* push in front of you, otherwise the first serving would have gone to Ongar Manganian, just as he said. And then later, just as Roddy collected the servings for Lexie and Tristram, I noticed that you two had nearly finished. I was expecting you to come up for second helpings momentarily—"

"So you think someone could have tampered with the food, not once, but twice?" He shook his head. "The only one who could have done that was someone behind the table, serving . . .''

"No!" It was impossible to believe. Gretel could have made one mistake of some kind, but would she have repeated it later that same evening? It was in Nick's best interests to see that everything went smoothly. And Mona? No, angry and upset though she had been, Mona would never deliberately poison the food. Not even to get even with Nick.

"No," I denied again. "It couldn't have been one of us."

"I agree." Ongar Manganian had come up behind us. "My enemies could not have suborned one of you so easily. There must be another explanation. Perhaps when we are allowed to visit the patients and question them—" He glared around unhappily. "Why are we being kept waiting for so long?"

"It takes time to pump out three stomachs," Aldo said. "And the patients are going to be rather weak and unhappy for a while. I shouldn't imagine they'll feel much like talking."

"And the laboratory? Why have we not heard from them? They know where to reach us?"

"It takes time." Again Aldo tried to soothe him. "They don't know what they're testing for. Unless something shows up right away, it will mean a long series of tests to work through all the possibilities. It could take all night. All morning," he corrected himself.

Already, dawn was streaking the sky and birds were fluttering and chirping in the trees of the square outside the hospital.

"Call them and ask for a progress report," Ongar ordered. "The very poisons that have been ruled out may tell us something."

Aldo tensed. For a moment, I thought he was going to tell Ongar to do it himself. Then he shrugged and smiled down at me. "I'll be right back," he said. But before he could leave, a nurse entered.

"If you'd like to see your friends—" Without hesitation, she marched up to Ongar. She had obviously been briefed as to who was paying the bills. "You can go up for a few minutes now. But you mustn't stay long. They're still quite weak."

We wheeled in a body and rushed for the door.

"I didn't mean *all* of you—" The girl tried to block our exit, but she hadn't a chance. Ongar Manganian shouldered past her with a grunt. Aldo caught her as she stumbled and set her to one side.

"I will speak to the doctor!" Ongar thundered back over his shoulder. "Have him come to me!"

We crowded into the lift and Aldo pushed the button for the third floor, where our casualties occupied adjoining rooms. We faced the front, silent and grimly attentive as the lift trundled upwards, not sure what we'd find when we got there.

Lexie and Humpty were together. Humpty lying back in bed; Lexie, obviously visiting, huddled in a hospital blanket in the chair by his bedside. They looked at us accusingly as we burst into the room.

"My poor, poor darlings!" Lady Pamela swept forward. "How *are* you?"

They ignored her. Humpty looked from Nick to me and drew a deep breath.

"You might as well know," he said. "We intend to sue!"

Chapter
18

That froze any expression of sympathy on our lips. There was no question now of sympathizing, far less of apologizing. I stared at them incredulously. I knew Humpty didn't like me, but . . .

"Lexie," I said faintly. "Lexie, you can't mean it!"

"I'm sorry, Jean." She wriggled uncomfortably, clutching the blanket more tightly round her as though she would like to pull it over her head and disappear into it, but the set of her jaw was stubborn. "Humpty thinks we ought to."

"Humpty—?" But he was still settling his grudge against us for ejecting him from the reception he gatecrashed. There was no quarter there.

"It's just not good enough." He glared back at me implacably. "You can't do this to people and expect them to take it lying down."

"Oh, really!" Sidonie strode forward, looking as though she would like to shake sense into them both. Nick put out a restraining hand. "You can't *do* this!"

"We can, you know." Opposition seemed to be strengthening Humpty. "You can't go around feeding contaminated food to people and expect them not to mind. We've been *suffering.*" He looked around. "We're in *hospital.*" He shuddered. "We've had out stomachs pumped!"

I looked behind me for support, but Aldo had vanished. Ongar Manganian crossed to the bed, walking delicately, as though it might do further harm if he jarred Humpty or Lexie. He stood looking down at Humpty thoughtfully.

"I think you're rotten!" Sidonie was close to tears, her Charity Ball ruined, her first attempt at trying her wings dashed to the ground, and now a lawsuit pending, so that anyone who might have missed noticing what had happened would see it all rehashed in the scandal sheets. "Both of you!"

"See here—" Humpty blustered. There was getting to be too much opposition. "You can't talk to us like that!" He looked from Sidonie to Ongar Manganian, who still had not said a word. "See here—we have our rights."

Nick's fists clenched and this time it was I who put out a restraining hand.

"These people are your friends." Ongar switched his scrutiny from Humpty to Lexie. "Would you do such a thing to them?"

"They're not *my* friends," Humpty said. "People who purvey poisoned food aren't anyone's friends. They're a danger to the community. And," he added righteously, "the community needs to be protected from them. The public has a right to know what they've done."

"What does Tristram Quardon have to say about this?" Ongar demanded. He looked around. "Where *is* Tristram Quardon?"

"Yes," Lady Pamela said. "Where is your uncle?"

"He—" A tear formed and rolled down Lexie's face. "He's very bad. The worst of any of us. They're still working over him. They've transferred him to Intensive Care."

"Oh no!" Lady Pamela looked more thoughtful than shocked. "That's terrible!"

Humpty cringed as Ongar Manganian bent over him

abruptly. He snatched up Humpty's bellpush signal to call a nurse and began jabbing it repeatedly, his face grim.

"What is going on?" he barked at the nurse who appeared in the doorway, out of breath from her dash down the corridor in response to the urgent signals. "What are you doing with Tristram Quardon?"

"I don't know," the nurse gasped. She settled her cap and went on more decisively. "I thought there was an emergency." By now she had spotted the bellpush in Ongar's hands and frowned disapprovingly. "I thought the patient rang."

"There *is* an emergency," Ongar snapped. "I want to know what is happening to my friend."

"It's all right," Lady Pamela intervened. She was standing behind Lexie's chair. "It's perfectly in order to tell *us*. We're his closest relatives. We have a right to know."

"But I don't—" the nurse began.

"Enough!" Ongar interrupted her. "I will speak with someone in authority. Get me the doctor."

"Doctor is busy with his patient." The nurse was on surer ground. "He can't be disturbed."

The doctor was busy with Tristram Quardon. Fighting for his life. We digested the realization in silence for a moment.

"Very well," Ongar said. "Have him report to me as soon as he is able."

The nurse vanished and Ongar dropped the bellpush back on to Humpty's pillow. We were all lost in our own thoughts. I moved closer to Nick and Mona. If Tristram Quardon died . . .

Edda Price began to sob quietly. Roddy patted her arm awkwardly. There was nothing to say. Her world was crumbling around her for the second time in as many months.

"We'll be ruined," Mona choked. "*Ruined!*"

"I don't see what you're getting so upset about." Humpty was increasingly on the defensive. "After all, the insurance will take care of everything."

"It won't take care of our reputation!" Nick snapped. "You're putting us out of business."

"One moment!" Ongar Manganian held up a hand. "What is this about insurance? How much are you carrying?"

"We're not," Nick said. "I don't know where he got that idea—"

"*We* are," Sidonie said quietly. "The Charity Ball. We have the customary comprehensive cover. We're insured for everything from having to cancel because of bad weather, to someone's having an accident while on the ground, to—" Her voice broke. "To an outbreak of ptomaine poisoning among the guests due to the catering."

"And you say this is usual?" Ongar frowned.

"Yes." Sidonie seemed slightly surprised that he should question it. "It's a standard cover offered to charity organizers for garden parties, fêtes, balls, gymkhanas—"

"And how many people knew of this?"

"Why. . . why, everyone. There was no secret about it." Sidonie's eyes widened. "Lexie and I were laughing about it when I got the proposal form to fill out . . ."

"I see," Ongar said softly. The silence deepened.

There was movement behind me. Someone entered the room, closing the door firmly behind him. I turned to find Aldo by my side.

"I've just been through to the laboratory." He reported to Ongar Manganian. "They've run all the preliminary checks for all the obvious things and found nothing. They're still testing, as per orders, but they're willing to give odds that there's nothing wrong with the food."

Lexie disappeared into her blanket, but Humpty's mattress wasn't so obliging.

Mona hurled herself into Nick's arms, laughing in relief. He swung her around, lifting her off the floor, then set her down again and turned to face Humpty, his eyes blazing dangerously.

"See here—" Humpty pressed back against his mattress,

trying to brazen it out. "I'm willing to be reasonable. I'm perfectly prepared to settle out of court."

"*Oh!*" Her burst of indignation carried Sidonie across the room. She tore at the blanket cocoon sheltering Lexie and pulled it away. She managed to get in one rousing slap across her cousin's face before Lady Pamela caught her hand.

"That will be quite enough," she said coldly. "I think it's time Lexie went back to her own room and rested now."

"Yes." Lexie struggled forward, trying to fight free of the twisted blanket. "Yes, I'm very tired. And—" she tried for pathos—"I feel terrible."

Her bid for sympathy was wasted on the rest of us. We watched her coldly and she seemed to shrink back from the combined force of our gaze. Lexie never could stand disapproval and now she was facing open hostility for perhaps the first time in her life.

"I believe the young lady has some explaining to do before she leaves us," Ongar said. "It would be better that she begin now. Or—" He turned to Humpty, who was eyeing Lexie with no more fondness than the rest of us. "Or perhaps *you* would tell us?"

"Let Lexie tell you herself," Humpty said sulkily. "It was all her idea. Everything," he added bitterly, "was her idea."

"Everything?" Ongar seemed momentarily at a loss. He looked at Humpty uncertainly.

"There you are, Manganian!" The door flew open and a tall, thin man in a white jacket charged into the room. Two nurses hovering nervously in the doorway bore witness to his credentials—unnecessarily. Only someone at the top of his field would have the arrogance to savage the hand that fed him so lavishly. "What the hell are you playing at here?"

"Playing at?" Ongar swung to face the consultant. "What do you mean?"

"What do *you* mean?" the doctor countered. "I've just

had the report on the stomach contents. They were all perfectly innocent. What devious game are you—?"

"We know that." Ongar sounded almost apologetic. "There has been a terrible mistake."

"There certainly has. We've wasted valuable time and, worse, weakened a man who was in no condition to be weakened, before we discovered what was actually wrong with him."

"Tristram Quardon—" Aldo stepped forward. "What *is* wrong with him?"

"We're preparing him for emergency surgery now," the doctor said. "But he should never have had to go through the ordeal of having his stomach pumped. Who was responsible for giving us false information? I shall hold him personally responsible if the operation is unsuccessful!"

"What's the matter with Tristram?" Lady Pamela's voice rose unsteadily.

"His Pacemaker has failed." The doctor swung to glare at her. "We're replacing it immediately, but he's been put through added and unnecessary stress. He's not in the best of condition for surgery—"

"*Pacemaker?*" Ongar Manganian said unbelievingly. "Tristram Quardon had a Pacemaker?"

"Doctor—" One of the nurses spoke timidly from the doorway.

"Coming—" The doctor turned towards her, then swung back to glare at us all impartially. "I'll have words with you later, Manganian. Don't go away!" The door snicked shut behind him.

"Tristram Quardon has a Pacemaker?" Ongar repeated, still incredulous. "Why was I not told?"

Because Tristram Quardon was afraid it might count against him. Because he was afraid you might use the knowledge to further undermine his control of Quardon International.

"We . . . we didn't think it was important, Mr. Manganian,"

Roddy Bletchley spoke as timidly as any student nurse. "We didn't think it made any difference."

"*We* didn't think," Ongar Manganian mimicked him cruelly. "*We* didn't—! Who knew of this?" he demanded.

"Everyone," Roddy said. "Everyone who was around at the time," he qualified. "It happened nearly two years ago. He's been getting along so splendidly we'd practically forgotten it by this time. He was his old self again."

"*You* knew." Ongar glared at him. "And *you*." He switched his glare to Edda Price. "And—"

"We *all* knew," Lady Pamela cut in impatiently. "What difference does it make, for heaven's sake? Some people can go on for decades with their original Pacemaker. Tris has just been unlucky, that's all."

"Is it?" Ongar met Aldo's eyes. "But there are occasions . . . and places . . . that *do* make a difference when a man carries a Pacemaker within him. It is dangerous for him to enter an electronic field . . . to linger near a microwave oven . . ."

"Microwave! Oh no!" I felt dizzy, but there was nowhere to sit down. I would *not* sit on the edge of Humpty's bed. I leaned against Aldo instead. "I can't believe it."

"It is true," Ongar said. "In the United States, restaurants must now display signs: '*Warning. Microwave oven in use.*' I had already noticed that such warnings were not required here. Perhaps because the microwave oven had not reached such a peak of popularity. Or perhaps because there are not so many Pacemakers. Over there, the operation has replaced the appendectomy as a surgical moneyspinner. Better, because the appendix can only be removed once, but a Pacemaker can be implanted and replaced several times."

"The United States . . ." I echoed faintly. Automatically my eyes turned to Lexie. Lexie, who had learned so much on her famous trip to New York. Lexie, who had kept insisting that we really needed a microwave oven . . .

She was huddled back in her chair, the blanket clutched around her again, but she could no longer escape by withdrawing into it. Her face was pale and frozen, her eyes burned, defying us to prove anything.

"*Lexie* . . ." I whispered. "*No!*"

Sidonie shrank away from her, no longer ready to do battle with her, not willing to touch her at all now. Even her mother stepped back. Lady Pamela, who had earlier insisted, "You can tell us . . . we're his closest relatives."

His next-of-kin. Lexie, his heiress.

Once again, I saw that scene by the microwave oven. Tristram Quardon, frowning and uncomfortable, trying to move away. Lexie, putting her hand on his sleeve, not letting him go, holding him in range of the deadly microwave emissions . . . until the damage was done and he collapsed.

Then, coldly and callously, she had tried to throw the blame on us. She had claimed to be sick herself, thus setting the seal on our growing conviction that something was wrong with the food. She had carried through with the charade to the point of having her own stomach pumped in order to keep the doctors from discovering the real trouble with Tristram Quardon. The fact that they had pumped his stomach as well was an added bonus, further weakening him and endangering his chances under the surgeon's knife. With just a little more luck, they might not have learned about his Pacemaker until it was too late.

"I can't believe it," Edda Price said slowly. "Not Lexie! Why, from the time she was a little girl, she adored her Uncle Tris—" Her voice wavered and broke.

"But they grow up." Ongar Manganian sighed heavily. "Some grow up hungry; some grow up wicked."

Lexie had been hungry in a different way: money-hungry. She had grown up surrounded by friends who all had more money than she had and overshadowed by the knowledge of the inheritance due to her cousin. She must have watched Tristram Quardon with secret anticipation, especially over the last few years when it had become apparent that only a few beats of a faulty heart had stood between her and

Quardon International. But her uncle had gambled on having a Pacemaker implanted and the gamble had paid off. Until now.

Lexie always had been impatient.

"Don't admit a thing, Lexie," Humpty warned. "Don't say a word until you have legal counsel. I'm not going to." He pressed his lips together tightly and glared at us.

But he had already said too much. Earlier, before the full extent of the scheme had been realized. "*It was all her idea. Everything was her idea.*"

Edda Price was still shaking her head unbelievingly, but Roddy, I noticed was quietly backing towards the door.

"Well," he said defensively, as he caught my eye and realized that I had seen him. "Someone has to do something—"

And Roddy was always the person called upon to do it. Roddy, the troubleshooter. But need he rush so enthusiastically to do something about this situation? The rest of us were only just coming to terms with the enormity of it. It had not yet occurred to us that the proper authorities should be called in to deal with it . . . with Lexie.

"That's right!" Lexie gave an abrupt giggle that owed more to hysteria than to mirth. "Roddy will fix it, won't he? Roddy fixes everything!"

Aldo caught her meaning faster than the rest of us. But then, Aldo had not known Lexie as the rest of us had. He had never worked beside her . . . laughed with her . . . been charmed by her . . . even against our better judgements.

And there had always been an underlying enmity between himself and Roddy. He deserted me to block Roddy's line of retreat.

"That's right." Again, Lexie gave that shrill mirthless laugh. "Don't let him get away. Roddy fixed more than you know."

"Mark Avery." Ongar Manganian made the connection. Like Aldo, he was less blinkered than the rest of us.

Roddy always took care of everything. He would be able

to cross the wires of an electrical connection, for instance. And he had free access to all the offices. No one at Quardon International would have given it a second thought if they had seen him emerging from Mark Avery's office—after having left Mark Avery's battery-operated shaver to run its batteries into uselessness and splashed a pool of water where Mark Avery would have to stand to use the mains-operated shaver.

"I did it for you." Roddy looked at Lexie with something less than devotion. "For us."

But he had not acted alone; there was no question of his trying to shoulder all the responsibility. Although it was Roddy who had initially decoyed Tristram Quardon into the deadly microwave field, it was because of Lexie that the microwave oven was there. It was also Lexie who had come along to take her turn at keeping her uncle in the fatal area until the damage was done.

"*You* were lucky—" Lexie turned her malevolent gaze to Edda Price. "If Jean and Gretel hadn't made such a damned row about the cheese wire going missing—"

Edda retreated, one hand rising protectively to her throat. So she had been the intended victim. No wonder Roddy had tried so hard to convince us that Ongar Manganian had taken the cheese wire. With Edda dead, there would be that seat on the Board to fill again. This time, Roddy might have a better chance.

Also, with both Edda and Mark dead, Tristram Quardon would have first call upon their shares in the business. He could buy them at a preferential price and thus a great deal more control of Quardon International would pass to Lexie . . . after his death.

Aldo had Roddy in a firm grasp now. Lexie sank back in her chair, exhausted.

Humpty had begun shaking uncontrollably as the realization of the true state of things swept over him. He had been the real catspaw tonight. He had been promised a quick and easy profit for a feigned fit of food poisoning. He was not terribly bright and had no idea of the darker forces operating behind the cover he was providing. How could he, any more than the rest of us, have suspected the evil behind Lexie's laughing face?

"So . . ." Ongar Manganian sighed deeply and looked to his lieutenant. "There is nothing more we can do." He reached for the private telephone beside Humpty's bed. "It is time to set the official wheels in motion."

Chapter
19

There was too much oregano in the spaghetti sauce. Other than that, the meal was close to perfect. The best part of it, of course, was that I hadn't had to cook it myself. There is nothing quite so soul-satisfying as hearing crashes, screams and curses emanating from the kitchen and knowing that, whatever has gone wrong, you are not going to be expected to cope with it.

Not that there had been an inordinate amount of disruption; possibly the sounds I had heard were just part of the everyday routine in an Italian kitchen. No doubt I would become accustomed to it in due course.

"More Grappa?" Aldo enquired solicitously of the table at large.

"No, thank you." My eyes were still watering.

He poured more anyway and went round the table, his mother following him with the coffee-pot while they replenished glasses and cups.

"I'll burst if I have one more mouthful," Mona declared and indeed the seams of her dress were already straining. The meal wasn't entirely to blame, however. She and Nick were reconciled and blissfully happy, although not for the same reason. Nick was certain that Mona had capitulated completely and would now fall in with his plans, little realizing that she had stopped taking the Pill during her absence. ("By the time they're ready to start shooting," she had confided to me, "I'll be too big to fit in the frame. Nick will have to find someone else.")

"A toast." Ongar Manganian rose to his feet, holding his glass aloft and catching my eye. For a moment I thought he was going to say, "*To the happy couple*," which would have been too premature by half. I gave him a baleful look.

"To our enchanting hostess, who has provided such a delicious meal." He finished quickly, drained his glass and sat down again.

I relaxed. That had been about the only toast we could all drink to happily. With Roddy in custody pending trial, Lexie on remand and Humpty out on bail and waiting to be called as Queen's Evidence, the situation was still too fraught for too many of us for the merriment to be unrestrained.

Sidonie, I was glad to see, was looking better these days. Without the insidious undermining of Lexie's constant presence, always forcing a comparison between them, Sidonie was quietly blossoming. She might never be a beauty, but she would someday be a force to be reckoned with. Antonio, Aldo's electronics-wizard of a brother, was keeping close to her side, looking as though he would be happy to do the reckoning. She could do a lot worse.

Gretel was sparkling at the end of the table, laughing with Papa Uccello. The discovery of Lexie's perfidy, although shocking her, had upset her less than the rest of us—she had quickly discovered compensations. Within a short time of a tight-lipped Lady Pamela's removing Lexie's things from the flat, Gretel had moved into the vacant room. We had encouraged the move, for we knew Gretel would pay her fair share of the utilities and provide company for Sidonie and keep her from brooding too much. The arrangement was working splendidly. In the kitchen, too, she had improved almost beyond recognition as her confidence grew.

I had recently received a lyrical letter from Gretel's delighted father after she had been home for a weekend and proudly demonstrated her new-found ability. He had always known that apprencticing her to me would be far better for her than working as an *au pair* for unknown strangers and I had proved him triumphantly right. His little girl was now an accomplished lady, a perfect cook, a sparkling conversationalist—the stories she could tell! (I winced at that one.) And she had made so many fine friends! He added, in closing that his other daughter would soon be old enough to continue her studies in England and was already looking forward to joining us.

"Please—" Edda Price pushed back her chair and helped Tristram Quardon to his feet. "We don't want to break up such a lovely party, but I think we ought to be leaving now. He won't admit it—" she smiled fondly at him—"but Tris still tires easily."

That precise situation was still anyone's guess, but I wasn't going to worry about it. I had problems enough of my own.

"Gina—" Mama Uccello sank into the chair beside me and beamed at me. "It is so nice to see you, at last. I have heard so much. All the time, 'Gina, Gina, Gina' from my Aldo."

"Jean," I corrected weakly, sensing that I was fighting a losing battle. It seemed I had an all-purpose name which could be adapted to any nationality.

"Gina," she agreed happily. "My boys—they are useless in the kitchen. All the hopes we had of them—pfft! They go their different ways. But—" she smiled lovingly at Aldo, then at Antonio—"but they are good sons. They find the right girls. Our restaurant will flourish."

"Excuse me." Ongar Manganian leaned across me. "I do not think your son is so wonderful. He tells me he cannot gravel with me so much any more. It will interfere with his courting!" A warm squeeze of my shoulder told me that he was not angry with me.

"Aldo is right," Mrs. Uccello said. "When you find a good girl, you do not leave her for someone else to find. You are big man, big money—is easy for you to find another assistant."

"Perhaps, perhaps." Ongar nodded. "But where do I find one who will—" He broke off just short of indiscretion. While Aldo had maintained an amused and tolerant attitude towards his employer's gustatory paranoia, it was more than possible that Aldo's mother would not take kindly to the realization that her son had been used as a guinea-pig for suspect food.

"It is true," Ongar went on thoughtfully, "that I need someone here in England permanently to keep watch over my interests—and for this I have trained Aldo well. But perhaps . . ." He nodded sagely again. "I have been considering. The young Humphrey—he is not really bad, I think. Misguided, ill-advised, but there is something I find not entirely unlikeable about him—"

Perhaps he reminded Ongar Manganian of himself. He was big enough. I did not voice the thought.

"Not beyond redemption," Ongar decided. "When this is over, I have the notion to take him in hand. I believe he can be taught . . . moulded . . ."

Poor Humpty. From Lexie's catspaw to Ongar's. At least, the pay would be better. Also, a few years of testing food which genuinely might be poisoned ought to give him a more respectful attitude towards it. What was it about the punishment fitting the crime . . . ?

"That's *my* chair—" Aldo lifted his mother to her feet. "Suppose you go rescue your husband from the Nordic charmer. You know he was always a fool for Marlene Dietrich."

"Hah!" His mother aimed an affectionate cuff at his ear. "I Dietrich him!" She moved off resolutely towards Papa

Uccello and Gretel, while Aldo took his place beside me.

"Now—" Aldo caught up my hand complacently. "As we were saying—"

I found myself smiling back at him, while my mind continued along another path.

Before too long, I really must take up with the Uccellos the matter of the amount of oregano in the spaghetti sauce.